Seduction on the Sand

The Barefoot Bay Billionaires #2

Roxanne St. Claire

Cover art by Robin Ludwig Design Inc.
Interior formatting by Author E.M.S.
Seashell graphic used with permission under Creative Commons CC0 public domain.

ISBN-13: 978-1500685706
ISBN-10: 1500685704

Published in the United States of America.

Critical Reviews of
Roxanne St. Claire Novels

"St. Claire, as always, brings a scorching tear-up-the-sheets romance combined with a great story: dealing with real issues starring memorable characters in vivid scenes."

— Romantic Times Magazine

"Non-stop action, sweet and sexy romance, lively characters, and a celebration of family and forgiveness."

— Publishers Weekly

"Plenty of heat, humor, and heart!"

— USA Today's Happy Ever After blog

"It's safe to say I will try any novel with St. Claire's name on it."

— www.smartbitchestrashybooks.com

"The writing was perfectly on point as always and the pace of the story was flawless. But be forewarned that you will laugh, cry, and sigh with happiness. I sure did."

— www.harlequinjunkies.com

"The Barefoot Bay series is an all-around knockout, soul-satisfying read. Roxanne St. Claire writes with warmth and heart and the community she's built at Barefoot Bay is one I want to visit again and again."

— Mariah Stewart, New York Times bestselling author

"This book stayed with me long after I put it down."

— All About Romance

Seduction on the Sand

Roxanne St. Claire

Dedication

This title is dedicated to Cathy Woodcock Henderson,
a loyal reader, supportive fan,
and tireless member of the team!

.

Chapter One

Elliott Becker climbed out of the helicopter and strode across the beach without bothering to apologize for his dramatic arrival that unexpectedly halted a high school reunion. A lot of faces in the crowd stared back at him, all easy to read. Men narrowed their eyes in distrust because he was wearing a Stetson and arrived by chopper. Women ogled openly because, well, he was wearing a Stetson and arrived by chopper.

He cleared his throat, tipped his hat back, and applauded himself for choosing this reunion to start his search. His goal had nothing to do with Mimosa High, but this was an easy way to reach a lot of island residents at one time. And *easy* was the only way he rolled.

"I'm looking for a man named Frank Cardinale," he announced to the crowd that had gathered when his helicopter had landed on the sand.

From under the rim of his hat, he scanned the crowd, catching a quick movement in the back. Long dark hair fluttered as a woman darted away, moving with just enough purpose that her retreat couldn't have been coincidental.

No one answered his question right away, so he zeroed in on the lady who'd left. With some luck, she'd lead him right to Mr. Cardinale. And if there was one thing Elliott Becker had a ton of, it was luck. And money. And charm. And some damn fine looks. He was about to put all of them to good use.

He followed his instinct and the sway of wavy waist-length hair the color of coffee beans. In a sheer cotton skirt that clung to her hips and danced around her ankles, she made an easy, and lovely, mark.

She power-walked down the beach, away from the resort and the party, heading straight to the frothy white shore where the Gulf of Mexico swirled in low tide. Just as her bare feet reached the water line, she glanced over her shoulder, too quickly for him to get a look at her face. But he could easily see her narrow shoulders tighten and her long legs pick up speed.

Interesting. Maybe someone didn't *want* him to find the owner of the twenty acres in Barefoot Bay that he and his partners needed to close this deal. The plans to build a small baseball stadium and start a minor-league team on Mimosa Key were supposed to be secret, but he and his partners had already nailed down verbals on three plots in the northeast corner of the island. Word could have gotten out that they wanted that last twenty acres, even though the other landowners had signed nondisclosures. On an island less than ten miles long and three miles wide? Even scads of money didn't buy silence.

He matched her quickened steps. No, she wasn't out for a sunset stroll; she was running. Not literally. Not yet, anyway. But definitely moving away from Elliott for a reason. A reason he had every intention of finding out.

It didn't take more than a few long strides to catch up, but he stayed about a foot behind her.

"I bet you know where I can find Frank Cardinale," he said, keeping his voice low and unthreatening.

She didn't turn, pretending not to hear him.

"Otherwise, why would you take off like a twister in a trailer park?"

That slowed her step. In fact, it stopped her completely. Elliott felt his mouth turn up in a satisfied grin. The Texas drawl always got 'em. Of all the moves his military family had made, he'd lived in the Lone Star State for only a year, but it was enough to pick up a few expressions and work on the twang. And, hell, he looked excellent in a cowboy hat. Now if she'd only turn—

"I live in a trailer." Her words were nearly lost with the splash of a wave at her feet.

Shoot. Way to blow the first impression. "It's just a turn of phrase, ma'am."

"More like an expression of condescension and mockery."

"No, a way to say you're moving too fast, not an insult to your home." He took two more steps, close enough to notice how the late afternoon light made her skin glow and pick up a whiff of something flowery and pretty. "After all, home is where the heart is," he said. Not that he'd know, but he'd certainly heard that enough in his life.

"It's not for sale." She spun around, making her hair swing like a curtain opening to a stage play. "So get back on your fancy helo, cowboy, and leave me alone."

He blinked at her, still not fully processing the demand because, man, oh, man, she was pretty. No, she rounded pretty and slid right into gorgeous, despite the fire in whiskey-gold eyes and the daring set of a delicate jaw.

"What are you staring at?" she demanded. "Are you deaf or just dumb as dirt?"

"Blind. By your beauty."

"Oh, *puh*lease." She looked skyward and sighed. "Spare me the lines."

"That's not a line."

Her eyes turned into golden slits of sheer disbelief.

"Okay, it's a line," he conceded. "But in this case, it's also true."

"Did you hear me? It's not for sale."

Yeah, he'd heard her, and the statement was starting to make sense, considering he'd come to the barrier island for one purpose, and it wasn't to flirt with sexy brunettes on the beach. Not that he'd fight the inevitable, but his goal was to buy land, and these words were not what he wanted to hear, no matter how scrumptious the mouth that spoke them.

"Do you know Frank Cardinale?" he asked.

She crossed her arms, which was patently unfair considering what that did to her cleavage. "I *am* Frank Cardinale."

He snorted softly and didn't fight the need to examine her breasts further. 'Cause, hell, now he had an excuse. "Considering ol' Frank is in his eighties and a man, I'd say you have one hell of a plastic surgeon, Mr. C."

"Miss," she corrected. "Miss Francesca Cardinale." She squeezed her upper arms as if nature and good manners were telling her to reach out and offer a handshake but she had to ignore the order. "Frank was my grandfather. He's dead."

The lady wasn't married, and the landowner was dead. Meaning this little excursion to the remote island would be fast, easy and possibly quite fun. He refused to smile at the thought, but took off his hat with one hand and extended the other. "I'm very sorry for your loss. I'm Elliott Becker."

She didn't take his hand, but met his gaze. "I know why you're here. You're not the first person to come sniffing around the land. Although you're the first to drop down like you owned the place."

"Which I don't." But he intended to.

The thump of helicopter blades pulled his attention. There went Zeke, whisking away the woman he'd recently gone stupid in love over. Zeke had taken the chopper for the day, leaving Elliott with the task of finding Frank—er, *Francesca*—Cardinale to close the land deal.

"But you're not getting my land, Mr. Becker, so you better find another ride out of Barefoot Bay." She gave him a tight smile, which only made him want to see that pretty face lit up with real happiness.

"Maybe you could give me one."

"A ride? Maybe not." She took off, not even bothering to end the conversation.

"I can walk with you, then."

"No."

He fell in step with her anyway. "Can I call you Francesca?"

"Make that a hell no." She refused to look at him.

He kept stride. "So, what's your price?"

That got him a quick look and almost—*almost*—a smile of admiration. Of course. Women loved relentless men. In cowboy hats. With Texas twangs.

5

"My price is too high for you."

And money. Women *loved* money, and he had even more of that than charm and sex appeal. "Not to be, you know, immodest or anything, but cash really isn't an issue."

She stopped and closed her eyes, so close to a smile he could almost taste it. And, damn, he wanted to. "Good for you, but let me make this clear: I don't want to talk to you, walk with you, or sell you one blade of grass that I own." With that, she powered on, shoulders square, head high, bare feet kicking up little wakes of sand and sea.

Damn, those were pretty feet. Would be even prettier if they weren't moving so fast in the wrong direction.

"Course there is the fact that you don't, uh, actually *own* that land." He cleared his throat. "Unless you really are Frank Cardinale."

Her speed wavered, her shoulders slumped, and she let her head drop in resignation. "What do I have to do to make you go away?"

"Smile."

She slowly turned to him. "Excuse me?"

"Smile for me."

She did, like a kid being forced to say cheese.

"A real smile." He gave her a slow, easy one of his own, lopsided and genuine enough to melt hearts and weaken knees and remove any clothing that needed to go. "Like this."

For a second, he might have had her. He saw the flicker of female response, the ever so slight darkening of her eyes, the thump of a pulse at the base of her throat. "The property is not for sale, and please don't bother taking this conversation one step further because the answer will be an unmistakable, unequivocal, indisputable no."

"A hundred thousand?"

She practically choked. "What part of that didn't you understand?"

"The long, unspellable words might throw me, but I got the 'no' loud and clear." He winked. "A million?"

Very slowly, she shook her head.

Oh, for cryin' out loud, let's get this done. "Five million? Ten? Fifteen? Everyone has a price, Francesca."

Then her face relaxed and her lips curled up and her eyes lit with something that reached right down into his gut and sucker punched him. "Not for a billion. Which I doubt you have."

She started to walk away again, and he lost the fight not to touch her. Reaching out, he closed his hand over her elbow and stopped her, pulling her very gently toward him so he could turn over his trump card, low and sweet and right in her ear.

"I have two billion. And a half, to be precise. I'm willing to part with enough to buy your land, make you a rich woman, and celebrate over dinner together. Do we have a deal?"

A glimmer of amusement lit her eyes, as gold as the sunset behind her now. "Is everything this easy for you?"

He laughed softly, mostly at the truth of that statement. "Just about."

"Was it easy to become a billionaire?"

Disgustingly so. He went for a self-effacing shrug. "Mostly a mix of good timing, dumb luck, and my irresistible boyish charm."

"Really?" One beautifully arched eyebrow lifted

toward the sky. "Well, guess what, Elliott Becker?" She cooed his name, already softening. The *B* in billion usually did that when his world-class flirting missed the mark. "Your luck ran out, your timing sucks, and I don't find you charming, boyish, or the least bit irresistible."

Undaunted, he took a step closer and lifted his hand, grazing her chin. "Bet I can change your mind."

"Bet you can't." She pivoted and took off so fast, she kicked a clump of sand on his jeans.

Brushing it, he just grinned. "How much are you willing to bet?" he called out. "I put fifteen million on the table!"

She stuck up her middle finger and kept running.

Sweet.

The only thing Becker liked more than a sexy woman with attitude was a sexy woman with attitude *and* a piece of real estate he wanted. This could be a good time. Maybe not quite as easy as he'd thought, but sometimes *hard* could be fun, too.

Chapter Two

*D*on't *look back. Don't look back. Don't give him the satisfaction.*

Of course, Frankie looked. What red-blooded human female wouldn't? And the cowboy was already ambling down the beach in the other direction, as fine from the rear as the front.

Under the cowboy hat, long, dark hair brushed the collar of his T-shirt. Faded jeans rested casually on a stare-worthy ass, drawing every woman's eyes to narrow hips and long, lean thighs that took huge strides as he loped away.

But she was a sucker for shoulders and, son of a bitch, he had those for days. Broad, strong, muscular. Along with a killer smile and bedroom eyes and…a billion freaking dollars. No, no. Two and a half billion freaking dollars.

Hello, deal breaker.

Had he actually said *fifteen million* dollars?

That blew every other offer out of the water, and from by far the best-looking bloodhound to come sniffing after her prime property. But, like the others, he'd soon learn she was serious about not selling. The land belonged in the Cardinale family, and it would stay in the Cardinale family as long as there was blood in her veins and breath in her lungs. No man—not even one who no doubt got whatever he wanted from 99.9 percent of the female population—could ever make her break that promise to her grandfather.

He'd learn soon enough that Frankie was the exception to whatever rules got him through his charmed life.

With a quick glance behind her, she abandoned the event and any chance of playing more verbal volleyball with the cowboy billionaire. She'd been there long enough to introduce herself to the Casa Blanca spa manager and arrange a meeting, which had been her only goal at the reunion.

Happy she'd left her sandals in her truck, she headed home before the sun disappeared in the water. Well, not home. *Kind of* home. Temporary home. Home for the moment, which was supposed to be a week or two and had extended to three months now.

It *felt* like home a lot more than that high-gloss, high-tech high-rise in DC. How had this tropical island stuck in the middle of nowhere become her home? For the second time in her life, too.

Sure, the place was a lush, undiscovered gem glittering in the Gulf of Mexico. A few years ago, the hills and lakes of central Barefoot Bay had been lost among the more desirable real estate along the coasts. But ever since Casa Blanca Resort & Spa had been built along the shore, money had been dripping into this island. Or dropping in by helicopter, she thought with a mirthless smile.

It was like they'd gotten a newsflash when her

grandfather had died without a will. Well, too bad, suckers. Florida's probate and intestate laws were crystal clear, as was her extremely sparse family tree. She'd inherited the twenty-some acres of glorious tall pines and gently sloping hills…and all that was on it.

Coming around the last corner, she slowed down to brace for the sight of exactly what that entailed: seven goats, two dogs, a milking shelter, and a less-than-luxurious single-wide that Nonno had rolled onto the land after his house was wiped out by a hurricane a few years ago. Yep, oddly, inexplicably, this wretched little goat farm had become her home.

Not *so* inexplicable, she thought as she rolled up the dirt road. This was the very place where she'd taken refuge thirteen years ago when her world came tumbling down. On those bleak days in the fall of 2001, when the world mourned people they didn't know and she mourned the parents she'd lost, she'd loved the security and simplicity of the goat farm. It was sunny and easy, with sweet goats and precious Nonno to make her forget the ache of being an orphan. She'd loved it then, and she loved it now.

Only now, without Nonno, it was lonely.

As she rounded the last bend, her gaze froze on a black SUV parked in front of the trailer. Holy hell, would these bloodhounds never give up? *It's not for sale, people!*

Sighing, she did a mental count of the days until this could end. Nine. Nine days until the full ninety-day probate period would be over, and she could officially wave a property title in her name in the faces of these relentless developers. All of them. Even the ones with bedroom eyes and ride-'em-cowboy shoulders. Shoot, was this *him*?

The thought rocked her as she slammed on the brakes next to the SUV. Had Wile E. Coyote somehow *beaten* her here?

She shoved her bare feet into sandals, trying to stomp away the tendril of heat and anticipation. Surely she wasn't going to be *that* girl...the one who went all breathless and giddy at the sight of a sexy rich guy. Not a chance in hell.

She threw open the door to hear Ozzie and Harriet from inside the mobile home, their high-pitched barks welcoming her home. Not the warning snarl of a Rottweiler that she *should* have to keep these idiots away.

Stepping out, she scanned the pen first to be sure all the girls were safe. Four of her goat does were visible, all offering their own distinct bleats to alert her that something was wrong. Still, no one was in sight. Was he around the side in the buck's pen? Maybe Billionaire Becker was stupid enough to let a horny male goat out of his gate? That might actually be amusing.

"Hey, where are you?" she called out.

"Don't take another step."

She froze, inching back at the low voice, searching side to side but unable to see who'd issued the warning. Someone with a serious amount of balls.

"I mean it." A man stepped out of the milking shelter that ran along the back of the pen. A man who was definitely not Elliott Becker.

Not nearly as tall, and wiry thin, the man wore a beige polo shirt and sported thin hair flopped over to cover a bald spot. Before she could get out a word, he held up a phone as if he were taking a picture of her. A wannabe landowner, of course. These nine days could not pass quickly enough.

"What the hell are you doing?" she demanded.

"I'm afraid you can't come any further, ma'am."

"Excuse me?" Was this a joke?

"You're on private property."

"I sure as hell am. *My* private property." She plowed toward the pen, ignoring the happy greetings from her goats. "Who are you and what are you doing on my farm?"

Inside the pen, he approached the gate, reaching it at almost the same time she did. His eyes were pale blue behind wire-rimmed spectacles, giving her no smile as he shot out his hand to deliver a business card.

"I'm Michael Burns, attorney-at-law and the personal representative with full power of attorney on behalf of the owner of this land."

She almost choked, closing one hand over the metal gate, the other automatically taking his card. "I don't have a personal representative."

"You're not the owner."

A little white spark of anger blinded her for a second, stealing her breath with its power. "I am—"

"Not the owner," he interjected, reaching to his back pocket to remove a piece of paper folded in threes, as though it had been in an envelope. "My client, Island Management, LLC, owns this property and has sent me to clear it off so it can be sold. I'm afraid you'll have to take your animals and find another place to squat, ma'am."

There were so many ways to respond to that, she couldn't even grab hold of one because nothing made sense. Island Management? Clear it? "*Squat*?"

"Technically, that's what you're doing." He gave the paper an officious snap to open it. "I have here the Last

13

Will and Testament of Francesco Antonio Cardinale."

She blinked, digging for anything that could be an explanation as she opened the pen gate and stepped inside, her grandfather's voice a soft echo in her head.

I no have a will, piccolina. I came to the world with no birth certificate and go out with no will.

The next breath got stuck in her throat, leaving her speechless. "No, that's not..." *Possible.*

Or was it? All she could do was shake her head and steady her hands as she reached for the paper. Words swam as she tried to make sense of them, a slow pulse pounding in her ears.

"That's his signature, a legal witness, and the seal of the great state of Florida." He pointed to the embossing at the top of the page, but Frankie's gaze stayed riveted on the signature.

Don't need to sign a will, piccolina. What's mine is yours.

And he'd been right...except not if there *was* a will. Was that possible, or was this particular shyster just incredibly creative?

"Who is Island Management, LLC?" she asked, absently closing the gate behind her because Clementine was already pressing her little white nose closer.

"I can't say."

"You can't..." She looked up, those white flashes of fury blinding again as everything suddenly fell into place.

The billionaire cowboy, of course. Forget beating her to the property—he'd beaten her to the punch. Somehow.

Oh, she knew how. Money can buy anything. "Don't tell me. Island Management is owned by an egotistical, smart-ass hotshot in a helicopter named Elliott Becker."

"I'm not at liberty, nor am I required by law, to reveal my client's identity."

Disgust and anger roiled up, matched by the sound of Ozzie's endless bark and Harriet's desperate whines for Frankie to come and greet them. Next to the man, Clementine and Ruffles bleated softly, staring up at him like they were actually following the insane conversation.

Then all those sounds disappeared at the purr of a motor and the crackle of tires spitting dirt in the distance.

Turning, Frankie wasn't even surprised to see a sleek silver sedan worth more than all twenty of the acres she was clinging to barreling onto her land. Coming in to hammer a nail in the coffin, Billionaire Becker? Oh, man, it was going to be fun to take this bastard down a few pegs.

Except, what if Nonno *had* signed a will? No. No, she refused to let herself even entertain that possibility.

"Oh, look, here's your client now." Still holding the paper, she whipped open the gate to go back out to the yard. Then she sucked in a slow, deep breath to be sure she had enough air in her lungs to give him holy hell. A strong hand clamped on her elbow.

"No one sent me," the lawyer said. "Hold it."

She yanked her arm free. "I know what this is about. Good guy, bad guy. You're going to play hardball with some fake"—she flicked at the paper—"piece-of-crap forgery, and he's going to throw insane amounts of money around. But trust me on this, neither one of you will get a thing."

The sedan door opened and, sure enough, Elliott

Becker emerged, this time without his stupid ten-gallon hat. Which, God help her, only made him more attractive. He stared at them, his head angled as if he were sizing up the situation. Wondering if she'd caved yet, no doubt.

"It won't work, Becker!" she called.

Behind her, the other man grabbed her again. "Who is that?" he demanded.

He didn't know? She threw him a surprised look and attempted to wrench her arm out of his grasp, but he held tight. "Let me go, asshole!"

"Hey!" Elliott's voice boomed across the farm as he strode forward. "Let her go."

Oh, yeah, good cop, bad cop. She wasn't falling for it.

"You're trespassing," the man behind her barked.

True enough, but…they really didn't know each other? Frankie looked from one to the other, then tried again to free her arm. "Let go of me!"

When he didn't, Elliott charged closer, hoisting himself over the fence in one smooth move. "Get the hell off her," he ordered through gritted teeth.

Clementine snorted while Agnes and Lucretia, the wee pygmy goats, trotted closer like kids on a playground attracted to a fight.

"You know this guy?" Elliott asked without looking at her.

"Don't you?"

He threw her an incredulous look. "I landed on this rock less than an hour ago. Is he hurting you?"

The anger and protectiveness in his voice touched her, but she squelched the female reaction. "He just showed up here with"—*phony papers and lies*—"threats."

Elliott's eyes tapered even more as he practically breathed fire at the smaller man. "Get out of here."

"I have business with Miss Cardinale."

"Business to maul her?" he fired back, looming over the man. "Do you want him to leave?"

"Yes." She wanted them *both* to leave.

"Get out." He got his chest—a big, mighty, impressive as hell chest—right in the smaller man's face.

"I have a legal docu—"

Elliott reached out and closed a sizable fist over the guy's collar, jerking him toward the gate. "Get the hell out."

The other man's eyes widened as he fought to keep his composure. "Fine. Let me go."

Elliott didn't move, his nostrils flaring.

"Let me go," the lawyer said again. "And I'll leave."

Very slowly, Elliott opened his fingers, and the lawyer tried to shake off the contact, brushing his polo shirt.

Elliott leaned in to make his point. "If you ever lay a hand on this woman again, you will regret it for the rest of your life."

The threat hung in the air, until Arlene let out a long nay and nuzzled her flat nose into Elliott's thigh. She might as well have sighed, "My hero!"

"You can keep that paper, miss," the lawyer said as he opened the gate to leave the way normal men did. "The old man signed two copies, and I have the other one. You have exactly nine days to get yourself and your stinky animals off my client's land."

He walked away before she could react, but Elliott whipped around and looked at her. "What did he say?"

"You really don't know him? You really didn't send him?"

He gave her a shake of his head.

She stuffed the business card into the twisted wire of the gate like a little white flag of surrender. "Then you just became the lesser of two evils."

Chapter Three

When the SUV disappeared around the bend, Elliott finally took a moment to drink in exactly where he was. In a cage full of strange-looking animals. Two no bigger than a medium-sized dog, and the bright orange one stuck its nose in his belly and started to bleat like a...

"Are these...nanny goats?"

"These are does," she replied. "The buck is in another pen around there."

"And that's, like, a billy goat?"

"Only if you are a graceless clod. No one with any real class would call them nannies or billies unless you are referring to meat goats. Mine make milk and soap." She closed her eyes as if an adrenaline dump hit her system. "I guess I should say thank you for getting rid of him. He was peskier than most."

She raised goats? And scoffed at a legit offer of a million? More? He inched back, taking another look at her frilly skirt and sandals, the wild-from-the-wind long hair, and the natural cream of her skin, sizing her up in a second.

A hippie chick earth mother who might be hot as

Hades but surely could be bought. Maybe a million didn't make her go all gooey and send her on a beeline for the mall like most women, but a sweet little donation to her cause *du jour* and enough cash to take her critters to another farm? Easy peasy.

All righty then. Game on, goat girl.

He slipped his hands into the pockets of his jeans and tipped his head to look a little modest and respectful. "So, what was that all about, if you don't mind me asking, ma'am?" He held out his hand in a quick correction. "Not that you look like a *ma'am*. Can I use your first name? Francesca?"

"Frankie," she corrected absently, focused on the paper she held. "This can't be real."

"May I?" He reached for the document, their fingers brushing in the exchange, allowing him to feel the tension in her knuckles. "Relax," he said softly. "He's gone."

"For now."

"I won't let him hurt you."

"I hate to break it to you, big guy, but I probably could have handled one wormy lawyer with a bad comb-over. But that paper?" She curled her lip at the document. "That's a little scary, because my grandfather didn't have a will."

"This would say differently." He scanned the words, simple enough to follow: Frank Cardinale had left his property and everything on it to Island Management, LLC. "Do you know what that company is?"

"Don't have a clue. Do you?" There was enough accusation in her voice that he knew she suspected he did.

He shook his head, rereading the document. If this

was real—and it sure looked legit—the person he should be negotiating with was that lawyer he'd just tried to punch, not the lady and her Billy Goats Gruff. "Didn't you say you had other interest and offers on the land?"

"Plenty of interest, and I just ignore the offers. I have no plans to sell." Next to her, a brown and white goat with massive ears nuzzled into her waist, and she stroked its head, the only noise the incessant barking of dogs inside.

He gestured toward the trailer. "You want to get them?"

"They'll settle down," she said. The goat next to her nayed again, pushing Frankie harder while another—a miniature with a twin—did the same on her other side.

"I know, I know, ladies," she cooed, rubbing their bodies. "I'll take care of you in a minute."

Elliott handed back the paper. "What are you going to do about this?"

"I don't know." She crouched down, face-to-face with the orange goat, reaching under its belly before looking up at him with a disarmingly pretty smile. "But first I'm going to milk my goats. You can leave anytime or…watch."

Holy hell, that sounded…unappealing. "By all means, milk."

She stood and nudged the animal toward the back of the pen, to a long, enclosed wooden structure with no doors and square holes for windows and a corrugated tin roof. "I have to do this every twelve hours whether I want to or not. That's my life now." A mix of irony and humor tinged her voice, piquing his interest.

He followed her, another goat at his side and two

more behind her, fuzzy, noisy, curious little things that had no sense of personal space.

"So you're, like, a goatherder?" he asked.

As she stepped into the building, he heard her laugh softly. "Just like one."

He followed her in, his eyes adjusting to the dim light, his nose swamped with the musty, earthy smell of hay. Bales of the stuff were piled to the rafters of the wooden structure, filling up half of it. The other half was much cleaner, with a tile floor and a small kitchen-like area with a sink, cabinets, and an industrial-size fridge.

"You can sit by the milking station." She indicated a bench under a window that let in the last of the fading light and some fresh air. The bench faced a contraption that looked like a long wooden chair with a hole in the seat. One of the goats walked up to it, then turned to stare down Elliott.

"Hi." Elliott bent over and looked into two massive brown eyes and big teeth bared in a... "Is he smiling at me?"

She let out a sharp laugh as she wove her fingers into her hair and started sliding one strand over the other. "*He*? I'm about to milk *her*."

"Oh, yeah." Elliott settled on the bench not far from the goat, much more interested in the other female in the place. She faced him, her hands still busy with her hair—braiding it, he realized—with deft, swift hands. The position showcased a narrow waist and nicely round breasts that he had to force himself not to examine too obviously. "I don't know much about goats," he admitted.

"You don't say." She turned to the sink to wash her hands, and then opened a drawer, pulling out a box of

22

latex gloves and an array of stainless steel equipment that she placed on a tray with easy grace.

With her back to him, he was free to take in every curve of her feminine form. The long braid settled down the middle of her back, pointing to a sweetly shaped backside. She tied an apron around her waist and turned, catching him staring at her.

"You don't look like a goatherder," he observed.

As she carried the tray to the contraption where the goat waited patiently, she fought a smile. "Just goatherd. You don't say shepherd-er, do you?"

He didn't say either one very often. "I didn't even know people still owned goats. I thought they were at petting zoos and in kids' books."

She laughed again, a sweet, musical sound that made him only want to hear more, as she got her pretty face close to the flat-nosed, floppy-eared goat. "You are so misunderstood, aren't you, Ruffles?"

Straddling a small bench so her skirt fell to either side, she placed a bucket and patted the platform next to her. "C'mere, girl, and let's do this."

The goat let out a long staccato nay and then ambled into place, jumping up a foot or so to get her hind legs over the hole where the bucket was.

"I'm going to guess you've never seen anyone milk a goat before," Frankie said as she snapped on a pair of gloves.

"Or a cow."

She looked up, surprise in her eyes. "With that hat and accent? I figured you just walked off the range."

Busted. "City Texan," he admitted. "Big difference." The year they'd lived in San Antonio hardly qualified him as a real Lone Star Stater, but he'd gotten his use out of it.

The goat bayed again as Frankie's hands started to squeeze and stroke, followed by the sound of liquid splashing into the stainless steel bucket.

"There we go," she whispered into the goat's ear, adding a soft kiss. "That's the dirty part, Ruffles."

She pushed back and dragged the bucket out of the way, then replaced it with a fresh one. Her feet hooked under the bench as she leaned forward, serious now, the muscles of her legs visible through the thin skirt. With spare, confident movements, she stroked the goat's...udders? Teats? He had no idea what a goat rack was called and wasn't about to amuse her any further by asking.

"Nonno was a little confused before he died."

The statement threw him, coming from nowhere and yanking him back to the real business at hand—who really owned the land he wanted.

"Your grandfather?" he guessed.

She nodded.

"Confused enough to sign a will you didn't know about?"

She sighed, her fingers squeezing and moving like a well-practiced professional. He sat stone still and watched the choreography, mesmerized and suddenly, surprisingly uncomfortable. Damn, who would have thought a woman milking a goat would be sexy?

"Do you think the will might be legitimate?" he asked.

She didn't answer for a long time, concentrating on her goat. "I guess anything is possible, but unlikely." She looked up, a single strand of dark hair that had escaped her braid slipping over one eye. "For example, you showing up at exactly the same time as this lawyer with a fake will. Why did that happen in the same hour if you aren't teaming up on me?"

"We're not," he said honestly.

"Then that's one hell of a weird coincidence. Which, by the way, I don't believe in."

"I do."

She snorted softly. "Well, I don't."

"Coincidence, karma, good fortune or lady luck, whatever you call it, I happen to be a living, breathing believer in it all," he said, leaning back and crossing his legs. "And my guess is the universe is trying to tell you it's time to sell this land. To me."

The fire in her eyes damn near fried him. "The universe is not telling me a damn thing except to stay away from smarm-fests like that lawyer and…and…"

He grinned. "I can't wait to hear how you describe me."

A slow, deep blush gave away how right he was. "How do you know what I'm going to say?"

"Your eyes. They're eating me up trying to come up with something insulting, which, of course, you can't."

She choked a hearty laugh. "And egotistical, arrogant, entitled billionaires. How's that?"

He answered with a shrug. "I've heard worse. On the beach an hour ago, as a matter of fact. From you."

"What you didn't hear, obviously, is this: My property isn't for sale."

"It might not even be yours."

Her hands froze, and tension tightened her shoulders. "It's mine."

But was it? "Are you sure your grandfather didn't make some kind of backdoor deal you didn't know about? I have to admit, it wasn't easy to find any record of him alive or dead when we were tracking this property."

She made a face but didn't reply, her hands moving a little faster to wring milk out of poor Ruffles. After a few minutes, she backed off, and he could have sworn the goat sighed with relief.

"All done, Ruff." She swatted the goat's backside and scooted her off the platform, twisting to pick up the bucket and carry it to another tray. "Clem, you're up!" she called, and another one, a little smaller and almost all brown but for a spot on her forehead, ambled over for her turn at the station.

"How long have you been doing this?" he asked.

"Eighty-one days."

Eighty-one days, twice a day, with half a dozen goats? "No wonder you're such a natural."

She worked on the next goat in line, repeating the same series of actions she had with the first animal.

"It's not that difficult." She swiped that stray hair with the back of her gloved hand and then blew out a long, slow breath. "And as far as my grandfather, he was never big on paperwork. He used to say he was born without formalities and he'd die without them, too."

"No one is born without some sort of paperwork," he said.

"Nonno was. He was born in a farmhouse in Italy, and they didn't bother with a birth certificate."

"Not a town record?"

"He did have a baptism, and that was logged in a local church, but they weren't sure how old he was then. Best we can tell, he was eighty-eight, maybe eighty-nine when he died."

"How long ago did he die?" he asked.

26

She stopped milking for a moment, closing her eyes. "Eighty-one days." The pain in her voice was undeniable.

"Oh, wow. Really sorry." And this time, he meant it. But he couldn't help assessing the situation with this new information. She'd been here only since he'd died, which could mean she had no idea if that will was real or not. "Were you close to him?"

"Not close enough," she murmured, inching closer to her goat.

"But you are his next of kin? Or would that be one of your parents?"

"My parents are both dead," she said quietly. "And I was Nonno's only relative, so the land belongs to me." She finished this goat and turned to Elliott. "It's a very clear-cut law in Florida when a person doesn't leave a will. I've already looked into it and talked to the County Clerk when I moved back here. That guy, that lawyer? He's a fraud."

But if Island Management really *did* own this piece of property, that's who Elliott needed to be doing business with, not the gorgeous goat girl. Sad, but true.

"You know," he said softly, trying to lessen the blow of the truth. "Your, uh, Nonno wouldn't be the first elderly citizen to get scammed when they were sick, dying, and had no will."

She closed her eyes with just enough misery for him to know he'd hit the mark. "That lawyer's just more imaginative than the other people who want this land. My property is desirable, as you obviously know." She stripped the gloves off slowly. "What are your plans for it? Hotel? Condos? Planned retirement community?"

Worse. He knew without a shadow of a doubt that

she'd hate what he and his partners were planning. A minor-league baseball complex? No, that would never fly. And if the lawyer was a fraud, Elliott would still have to buy the property from this lady who would no doubt recoil when she found out her little goat farm would be turned into an access road and parking lot.

"Don't tell me," she said with a laugh when he didn't reply. "You're an eccentric, unhappy, lost, and lonely billionaire who has decided to reconnect with Mother Earth and wants to live on a working farm."

Bingo. Answer supplied. "How'd you know?" He managed to keep all humor out of his voice, earning a surprised look from her.

"Seriously?"

"Well, all except for the lonely part. I can usually scare up a date."

She rolled her eyes. "I bet you get plenty lucky."

"I told you, I am—"

"Lucky, yeah, I got that a few times. But I'm not—"

"Selling, yeah, I got that a few times, too." He pushed off the bench, impatience growing. Maybe she was just hardballing for the best offer. It's what he'd do. "I want the place," he said, leaving no room for argument. "I'll double your best offer."

"No, thank you." She stood, shoulders square, eyes narrowed, feet apart. Damn, she looked good mad. "I am not interested in money."

"Then how about I put that entire amount, and another few million, into..." What would be her soft spot? Something with animals. "Your favorite...goat charity."

"A *goat* charity?"

"Don't tell me, that's the wrong word. Shoot, I'm trying to make this painless for you, Frankie."

"Painless? *Painless*?" She took a step forward, as if she were about to induce some pain of her own. "You don't know what you're talking about, cowboy. The pain happened when the only family I had left died in my arms. You're just an...an..." She swatted the air like a fly had buzzed her. "An annoyance."

"I'm sorry about your grandfather, Frankie."

She glared at him. "Here's what you should be sorry about, Becker. I made my grandfather a promise. This land, these twenty measly acres of scrub and swamp, is going to stay in this family no matter what. And I will raise goats and make milk and soap and cheese for as long as I'm capable of it because that's what he wanted. Do you know what a deathbed promise is?"

One based entirely on emotion, which was just stupid when it came to land. "One you won't break."

"Finally, something you know." She blew out a breath like she'd been holding it for ten minutes, ignoring the next two goats bleating for their turn on the table. "Trust me when I say that no amount of money is going to take this land out of the family. No amount. So do us both a favor and leave." She pointed to the door and held the position for a good fifteen seconds.

He could change her mind. With sweet talk and a few promises of his own. He knew his power with women. But why bother? If the lawyer had a will, then, in nine days, the lawyer would have a deed. Becker's business wasn't with this woman, no matter how attractive she was. They needed her land to build *his* dreams.

"I'll show myself out," he said, stepping away and to the door.

Outside, the late daylight had faded, and twilight had descended over the goat pen. He kept an eye on the grass and dirt in case he might step in literal shit instead of the stuff he'd just walked away from.

He stole a look over his shoulder, a little disgusted at just how much he wanted her to be standing in the doorway, calling him back, asking for help. Which was moronic. She couldn't have made her aversion to him any clearer.

He reached for the gate latch, his gaze landing on something white wedged into the wire. *Michael S. Burns, Attorney at Law.*

Of course the business card would be there for the taking, because Becker's luck made his life easy. He snapped it up, climbed into his rented Audi, and had the guy on the phone before he'd reached the end of her dirt road.

Chapter Four

Sunday afternoons were usually Frankie's favorite time of the week on the farm. Instead of the impending press of Sundaynightis that used to plague her up in DC, she relished the end of the week because she didn't dread the beginning of it.

No paperwork, bureaucracy, rules and regs, or unbearable office politics loomed the next day at a desk job she'd once thought could make her happy. In the three months since she'd slipped into this unexpectedly blissful existence, she'd come to think of Sundays as a gift.

She groomed the goats most Sundays, spending the day cleaning and trimming hooves or brushing their fur. And she talked to them because, hell, there was no one else around.

But today, Frankie was restlessly moving about the farm, starting chores but not finishing, picking up the hoof clippers, then getting distracted by the oils she used for soaps, not accomplishing anything but watching the dirt road and listening for cars.

It was if she *wanted* Elliott Becker to come back, which was just so lame it hurt.

"Crazy," she whispered, snapping her fingers to get Ozzie and Harriet into the goat shed with her. The dogs trotted inside, more at home on this farm than they'd ever been pent up in that downtown apartment. Just like her.

Inside, the dogs sniffed and wagged and looked up at her with curiosity, as if they still wanted to know who'd invaded their home with a brand new smell the day before.

"A bad man," she told Ozzie, his big brown eyes staring up at her like he followed every word. Australian terriers might be a little stumpy and slow, but they had brains. At least Ozzie did. The little short-haired wiener named Harriet didn't have the smarts, but she was sleek and sweet and pretty as a picture. All beauty and no brains. Kind of like Cowboy Becker, who wasn't even a cowboy at all.

"A fake man," she muttered as she finished cleaning out the last stall. "A pretend cowboy who's probably not even a billionaire and no doubt is lying about...everything."

Ozzie barked his response.

"And dumb as a box of rocks!" she added, swiping her hands on her jeans. "A *goatherder*. What kind of big, dense, lug nut even says something like that?" He was big, all right, and gorgeous.

She shook her head, closing her eyes, more than a little disgusted with herself for being swayed by his good looks. Frankie had never been that kind of female. Swooning over his heroics with the lawyer, flirting with him while she milked the goats, sneaking peeks at his pecs? What was wrong with her?

She guided the last of the does out to the pen, except

for Isabella. About six weeks ago, Frankie had realized the doe wasn't just fat—she was pregnant, though Nonno had left no record of how far along she was. Frankie guessed by feel that she was nearing her term, so she let Isabella sleep in her hay, no doubt dreaming of the love of her life.

"Let's go feed him now." Both dogs trotted after Frankie to take the walk to Dominic's private quarters, far from the girls in case someone who wasn't ready to breed went into heat. Being the Italian stud he was, Dominic would have fought his way over to the pen for some good times with the does. She'd seen his temper a few times, and without a doe in heat, he was getting downright nasty lately.

As they passed the back side of the trailer, Ozzie stopped, and both his little stick-up ears turned, like radar dishes seeking a signal. A fine chill waltzed up Frankie's spine as she stood still, listening for whatever had attracted Ozzie's attention. A squirrel? A rabbit? A...*man*?

Maybe not Becker. Maybe that lawyer?

That's why she was restless, she thought. Tomorrow she had to go to the County Clerk's office—oh, that would be a fun five hours in a place not unlike her old office—and figure out if a legitimate will had ever been filed. They'd never even checked for that when she was last there because Nonno had told her...

She swallowed hard. Had he *really* told her? Or was she fooling herself? Because she knew damn well a will *could* have been filed. It *could* be legit. She hadn't been with him for two years, both of them too stubborn to say they were sorry. And during those two years...

A slow, sickening heat turned in her belly as she

watched Ozzie listen even more intently while Harriet rolled around on something delicious-smelling, her little paws in the air, her white teeth showing in a dog smile.

Ozzie finally gave up the audio hunt and continued to trot to Dominic's shed. The old buck bellowed as soon as they reached his long, narrow pen, this one surrounded by much sturdier fencing than what the girls had. His shed was much smaller, too, more for shade than anything else. Dom needed far less attention than the female goats. All he required was food, water, and regular sex, which basically made him like every man on earth.

"Hey, big guy." She reached over the thick railing to give Dom's dark head a pat and stroke his horns. His golden eyes settled on her with no small amount of longing. Longing that, if not satisfied, could turn to downright fury.

"Gotta wait awhile for Agnes to be ready, okay? A week or two, best I can guess." Of course, Nonno had left no records of any of the goats' cycles or births. It was like he'd lost all interest after the hurricane, after Frankie had moved to DC.

She swallowed guilt and refocused on Dominic, who blinked once, his pink gums sliding into what she'd swear was a smile. She tunneled her fingers into his wiry fur and scratched, thinking of how happy Nonno had been when he had Dominic shipped over from Italy. When his plans for "La Dolce Vita" were in full swing, before they'd had their fight, before she'd been a complete and total idiot who needed to "find herself."

She scooped up grain and feed, poured fresh water in the trough, and fluffed his hay. Finished, she whistled for the dogs and trudged across the field, eyeing the tiny one-bedroom trailer through the eyes of the cowboy who'd been here yesterday.

Why couldn't she stop thinking about him? Okay, it had been awhile since she'd had anything that resembled a date. In fact, let's be honest, the ladies in her pen got more action than she did and they had to share the same guy.

That was no excuse for her obsessing about him and wondering what he'd thought of the humble place where she currently lived. Without knowing why the trailer was there, he probably thought Nonno was dirt-poor and she was "trailer trash" who'd swoon over a multimillion-dollar offer for her land.

Man, he couldn't be further off base. He so completely didn't know what he was dealing with. He was—

Sitting on the first step of the trailer.

Ozzie exploded in an outburst of sharp, loud, frantic barks, launching toward the stranger.

"Whoa." Elliott didn't even stand, reaching out a hand, which Ozzie immediately sniffed. Harriet scampered around, trying to get a piece, so he reached his other hand to her, getting a total tongue bath for his trouble.

"Hey, pooches." He looked up and grinned, like his sneaky, unexpected arrival was completely normal and welcome. "And goatherd. Not goat*herder*."

Nothing was normal and welcome—especially the way her knees weakened and the rest of her tensed up at the sight of him. Well, of course, she was shocked. That had to be why her body went into this state. Nothing else.

"You scared the crap out of me."

35

"You're vulnerable out here." He tipped his cowboy hat back so she could see his eyes glint with humor and then travel up and down her body with open male appreciation. "Not really safe for a woman as beautiful as you."

"You going to play that card now, Becker?"

He took off the hat and set it next to him on the step, but Harriet launched onto it like the brim was dusted with bacon bits. "Which card?"

"Vulnerable? Beautiful? Heroic? Who knows with you?"

With an almost imperceptible flinch, he leaned forward to give Ozzie even more love, his fingers seeming to know exactly how to calm the high-energy dog.

"Of course, you have your vicious guard dogs to protect you." Ozzie was practically rolled on his back now, with Becker's big hand tunneling the dog's fur for a rare and prized belly rub. Ozzie was toast, his tongue already hanging out, his stub of a tail vibrating with joy. Harriet jumped off the step with the hat locked between her teeth as she trotted around the end of the trailer.

"You may never see that hat again," she warned.

He shrugged. "I've got plenty."

"What are you doing here?" she demanded, fighting the urge to press a palm to her pounding heart, but not willing to let him know he had any effect on her at all.

"What can I say? I'm drawn to"—one more sweep with his eyes and, damn it, she felt heat rise—"this place."

"I didn't even hear you drive up."

"My point exactly." He finally gave up on Ozzie and leaned back on locked arms, a move that made his biceps…huge. Ozzie threw both front paws on Elliott's lap, letting out a demanding bark for more attention. Which he got from those incredibly large and surprisingly tender hands.

Oh, Frankie, come on! They're just hands.

"I have an offer for you," he said, squinting up at her with an irrepressible grin.

She puffed out a breath, dropping her head back to let out a grunt of sheer exasperation. How could she make him believe she didn't want the money?

"One week." He stood slowly, taking a step closer. "Let me stay for one full week."

Her eyes widened, because she certainly couldn't have heard that right. "Excuse me?"

"I need to know if this is what I really want and need in my life."

"And you want to, what, try out the farm life to see if it's for you?"

"Exactly." His lips curled up, revealing stunning, perfect, white teeth and a hint of dimples hidden in the whisker scruff that was probably created using a special Hollywood clipper to get that perfect two-day-old-beard look.

"Nothing about you is real, is it?"

He recoiled a little at the question. "What makes you say that?"

"You really are a fake."

She had him; she could tell he didn't know how to answer that.

"You'll just be whoever you need to be to get a job done, am I right?"

"Um, I'm a little more complicated than that."

She lifted her shoulders. "I think you're simple. In

every imaginable way." She started to walk past him, but he sidestepped and blocked her.

"Come on, Frankie. I really want to know more about this...goat life. I've been reading all about goats, all night. They're really quite a huge business and fantastic pets. I've been thinking about"—his gaze moved to the pen—"Ruffles. And..." He lifted his hand as if he were going to touch her, then dropped it, catching himself. "You."

Don't do it, hormones. Don't listen. Don't react. Don't go surging into high gear.

"Don't shake your head," he said. "You know the attraction is there."

"You're attracted to Ruffles?"

He laughed. "You can't deny it."

No, she couldn't. "All the more reason for you not to be here for a week." As if she actually needed a reason. But the idea...oh, Lord. Why did the idea appeal to her? Was she *that* lonely out here?

Yes.

"I won't bother you, Frankie, I swear."

"Too late for that."

"And I won't sleep...near you."

"Have you seen my lavish accommodations?" She gestured toward the trailer. "One bedroom and a lumpy sofa in the living room."

Undaunted, he looked around. "I'll sleep in the barn."

"It's not a..." She closed her eyes, hating the thoughts that played at the corners of her mind.

"You wouldn't have to be alone when creepy lawyers and other people who want this place come circling like vultures." His enthusiasm was infectious, she had to give him that.

And he was dead-on about the vultures. He'd surely get rid of them.

"And you wouldn't be lonely."

"I'm not..." She swallowed the lie. "I have plenty of company with seven goats and two dogs."

"And a lot to do. I'd be happy to help."

She had to laugh. "Why do I think goat's milk soap-making is not your forte?"

"Is that what you do here?"

"This week, I will be."

"I can help you make soap. I know a lot about soap. I use soap every day."

She didn't know whether to laugh, cry, or beg for mercy. What had she done to deserve this?

"You can't handle a farm, Becker. It takes...experience."

"Says the woman who's been here for eighty-one days."

"Eighty-two, and I lived here when I was a kid."

"You're still not safe out here alone, and you know it."

"Please." She waved him off, along with the sense that he was right. "I have a .22 rifle, and I am not afraid to use it."

He snorted. "That'll get the evil squirrels, Annie Oakley."

"It could stop someone."

"Didn't stop me."

Damn it, he was right about that. "Well, something has to." She managed to get by him, powering straight for the trailer door. She pulled it open, aware he'd followed.

"And you don't even lock your door," he chastised.

On the top step, she whipped around, a little taller than he was now. She used the advantage to glare down her nose. "I will from now on. Goodbye, Becker."

Ozzie barked, loud and sharp, making his displeasure at the word *goodbye* clear.

"She doesn't want me to leave."

"Yes, *he* does."

He exhaled and shook his head. "Clearly, I need lessons on farm management and...and animal husbandry."

"Science," she corrected. "It's known as animal science, and I have a degree in it."

"Which will make you an excellent teacher."

Ozzie kicked it up to a deafening yelp, no doubt loving this idea.

"Oh!" She blew out pure exasperation, at him, at Ozzie's relentless barking, at the situation. "Come on in," she said, holding the door open.

"Nice work, partner." He scooped up the little terrier and followed Frankie in so fast, she could feel the warmth of him at her back.

"It's an invitation to come in, not sleep here."

She closed her eyes and turned one way and then the other, the tiny trailer closing in. Or maybe that was him, six feet of unstoppable testosterone and determination who'd just filled it. She moved a few steps into the tiny kitchen, flipping on the faucet to quench an inexplicably dry throat.

"So what's your real game, Becker?" she asked as she reached for a glass. "You think you can distract me or change my mind somehow? You make a bet with someone that you could spend a week with me and get my land?" She turned and caught him looking at the dog in his arms, wide-eyed like they shared a secret.

Like she'd just hit the nail on the proverbial head. "Did you?" she demanded.

"No." He stroked Ozzie, shifting his attention from the dog to her. "I really am intrigued by…this. And you. And I think you shouldn't be alone until you…you figure out what you're going to do with this place."

She frowned at him. "I've got it all figured out. And no other buyer figures into it."

He nodded, still stroking Ozzie. She refused to look at his hands. Hands that could…oh, boy. She took a deep drink of water.

While she drank, he dipped his head closer and closer, like he was going to…put Ozzie on the floor. Her heart almost stopped. Oh, brother. He moved one inch and she'd thought he was going to kiss her.

Instead, he reached over her head for his own glass. "Why, thank you for offering, I'd love a glass of water."

She tried to duck away to let him get it, which was damn near impossible because he was so big and filled her kitchen with all his body and…hands.

Enough with the hands, Frankie!

"I still don't completely buy this you-want-to-live-on-a-farm business," she said.

"I don't either," he admitted. "That's why I'd like to try it."

"They have dude ranches for that kind of thing."

He filled his water glass, smiling.

"What?" she asked, seeing the smirk.

"You're not a dude, that's all."

"Oh, God." She leaned against the counter, half-laughing, half-sighing. "You really think you can flirt me out of my land? That you can woo me with cute

41

jokes and a drop-dead smile and a sudden interest in goats?"

He turned. "Drop-dead? I like that."

"Then why don't you?"

He just laughed and looked down at Ozzie. "She totally likes me, don't you think?"

The little traitor barked twice and wagged his tail.

"He speaks English," she said.

"Obviously." Elliott crouched down. "Talk some sense into your mom, will ya, bud?"

He barked twice again.

"What's that mean?" Elliott asked.

"Go away."

He laughed again, an easy, playful, masculine laugh that sounded…good. There'd been no laughing in this little trailer for three months. No flirtatious banter, no combustible chemistry, no sexy side glances, no…man. No laughter, no music, no connection, no…romance.

And yet she'd thought she was content here. Nearly content, anyway. Almost content. Wasn't she?

He put the glass to his lips, giving her only his profile. He drained the whole glass, his Adam's apple bobbling, like he'd walked miles through the desert. Well, he had trudged up here from far enough away that she'd never heard the car.

As much as she wanted to, she couldn't take her eyes off him. Good God, the man was a specimen and a half of perfection. And protection. A thick bicep with the shadow of a vein running through, strong forearms dusted with dark hair. Then she was back to his hand, curled around the glass, all tanned, long, powerful.

But she didn't really know anything about him at all.

From behind the glass, she saw him smile.

"What?"

"You have a camera?" he asked, lowering the glass. "'Cause it would be easier to take a picture, Francesca."

She felt a warm rush to her cheeks at the use of her full name. And being caught staring. "You're standing in front of me gulping like a hog." She forced herself to turn, leaning on the sink and looking away. "How'd you get so"—*built*—"rich?"

He chuckled as if he knew exactly what her real thought had been. "Told you already. Dumb luck."

She gave a scoffing grunt, pushing off the sink to go back into the living room. He followed, with Ozzie practically crawling up his jeans, of course. "Not buying it. Nobody's that lucky."

"I am." He sat in Nonno's old recliner, the first man—the first human—to sit there in three months. Pushing back, he popped the footrest with a loud snap. "Haven't been in one of these for a long time."

"No La-Z-Boys in the mansion?"

He grinned, getting comfortable and, of course, making room for Ozzie on his lap. "I might have to change that."

Didn't deny he owned a mansion, she noticed.

"Anyway, to answer your question, I bought a very valuable piece of property." He crossed his feet and looked at her from under thick lashes. "I paid forty-six thousand dollars for about six acres of land in western Massachusetts."

"And selling that made you rich?"

"Nope. I never sold the land and never will."

She eyed him, curious, watching his smile grow and his dark eyes dance.

"But the first time I put a shovel in the ground, I hit some stone. Beautiful gold stone."

She gasped. "You struck gold in Massachusetts?"

"Close enough. Goshen stone. Rare and desirable, and the amount I had on my land—land that I bought as a favor to my cousin who really needed to sell, I might add—netted over two billion dollars."

"Wow." It was the best she could do because, wow. That *was* lucky.

"I know," he agreed. "So I might be arrogant about a lot of things, but not my money-making skills. I literally fell into wealth, so it doesn't really change who I am, just how I live. And, yes, I gave my cousin a cut."

He searched her face, probably looking for the usual drool women have to wipe when they learn his net worth. A flicker of discomfort registered on his expression when she imagined what he saw instead. "I mean, I live well," he said slowly. "I have a—"

"Yacht."

His eyebrows lifted. "Sure, I have a pleasure boat."

"And a private jet."

"It makes travel easier."

"Multiple expensive homes."

He lifted one shoulder. "I like to stay in my own place if I can."

"Butlers and staff and, of course, some ridiculous collection like art or horses or…"

"Rare cars," he supplied. "I'm not going to apologize for how I live. I told you I was in the right place at the right time."

But, still, she knew all she had to know about him. He worshipped at the money altar, and she despised people like that. She learned at a tender age that when you put money in front of everyone else, the ultimate price is too high. Her parents paid that price, and it still hurt her to think about it. You can't love people and money at the same time or with the same intensity. One wins out, everytime.

"Look." She took a steadying breath. "I really appreciate your concern for my safety and your interest in goats and whatever else you're going to dream up to persuade me to give you access to...me. But I don't think this is going to work out."

He didn't move, except for his infernal petting of her dog. "It's the money, isn't it?" he finally asked.

She scowled at the question, not believing she was quite that transparent.

"You have issues with money," he explained.

Well, yes, she *was* that transparent. "Who doesn't?"

"Most women—"

"Hey, newsflash, Becker." She snapped her fingers three times. "I am *not* most women."

Charcoal-black eyes raked her, from face to body and back up again, just as smoky and sexy as a man could look. "I noticed."

Damn it, she hated the heat that generated. Two words. One look. And a couple of billion dollars. "I don't believe money buys you happiness."

"So says everyone who doesn't have it."

She managed not to scoff at that. "Money buys nothing but misery. Trust me, I know firsthand. *Misery.*" If her parents hadn't been chasing the almighty dollar...they'd still be here.

He finally smiled. "This is good, Frankie. Really good."

"What is?"

"This arrangement." He gestured to her and then to him, as though they had actually made an *arrangement*. "You can teach me about goats and farms and animal science, and I can teach you that you are completely wrong about people who have money."

Could he? Maybe someone needed to do that, otherwise, she was never going to fully heal from the pain of losing the two people she'd loved and needed so desperately. Without giving herself a chance to think deeper than that, she nodded.

"Okay, then." She put her hands on her thighs and pushed up.

"Can I stay?"

Ozzie let out four furious barks, as though he could answer for her.

"I have six sets of very dirty hooves waiting to be cleaned and trimmed. That's a total of twenty-four goat hooves, which means forty-eight toes that need your attention."

He frowned, making her wonder if the simple math threw him. "I thought you had seven goats."

"One's a buck and, trust me, you cannot handle him."

He pushed up from Nonno's chair and smiled at her. "You have no idea how I live for a challenge. If I clean all twenty-four feet, can I stay?"

"Their called hooves, not feet. And, we'll see."

He scooped up the dog like he weighed nothing. "Let's go, Wizard of Ozzie. Farmwork to do."

As soon as she opened the door, Harriet came bounding over with his cowboy hat in her teeth. Well, what was left of it. The brim was shredded.

Frankie bit back a laugh, but Elliott just hooted as he

put down one dog to give his attention to the other. "Would you look at that?"

"Sorry," Frankie said, fighting an outright giggle.

He gave her that slow, sexy, careless smile as he set the hat on his head and the ragged brim dipped over his forehead. "Let's get to the hooves, boss."

Damn it. *Damn* it. Did he have to be so stinking sexy?

Chapter Five

Elliott rolled over, a jolt from head to toe. Pain jabbed his back and something fuzzy scraped his ear. His forearms ached from compressing the damn shears, using every ounce of strength he had to snap off hard chunks of goat toenail. His thighs hurt from squeezing the beasts between his legs as he bent over goat butts and held their hind legs up to do the work.

Holy mother of misery.

Everything hurt and needed rest and a five-hundred-dollar massage and sauna at the club in Manhattan. Later. He'd make an appointment later. Now, he had to sleep, the need pressing his lids closed and numbing the pain. In his ear, a soft sigh pulled him a little further from a dream, and he reached out to...

He dug through sleep-fog for a name. Francis. No, Frankie. Fiery, feisty, funny, and...*furry*?

With a grunt, he threw himself backward, as far away from the little goat as possible.

Ruffles.

A musical laugh filled his ears. That pretty, girlie, bell-like laugh he hadn't heard nearly enough while he cleaned shit—actual, *real* manure—out of goat hooves. Shifting in the hay bed he'd made the night before, he squinted to see Frankie at her milking station, already wringing the crap out of Clementine's titties.

Holy hell, he knew their names. Plus, it couldn't be seven in the morning. Did it never end, this goat business?

Well, this was part of the deal he'd made with the lawyer, right? Burns had salivated at Elliott's offer and asked for one week to close the sale. During that time, Elliott had to make sure Frankie hit nothing but roadblocks until he and his partners owned the land. That required constant supervision and, evidently, sleeping in a goat barn.

"How'd you sleep?" Frankie asked, the splash of milk into a metal bucket not hiding the little note of concern in her voice. She might act like she didn't care that he had to sleep here, but she did.

"Like hell in a haystack." He leaned up on one elbow, scowling into early sunlight that streamed through the opening behind her, backlighting her so she looked...great. Really great. "You're up early."

"It's a farm, big boy. That's how we roll."

Too tired to argue, he rested his head and let his eyes focus on her. Jeans today, faded but tight enough to show every curve. And an oversized T-shirt so loose that when she leaned over to adjust the milk pail, he could see right down to a tank top. Her hair was pulled back in her Heidi braid. Small, taut muscles in her arms bunched as she squeezed out milk, her lower lip tucked under her teeth in concentration, a glisten of perspiration giving her a glow.

"You can use the facilities in the trailer," she said, not even looking at him.

"In a minute. I'm mesmerized by milking." And the milk maid.

She tried to hide her amusement by tucking her head under the goat's belly instead, but he caught the smile. "Good, you can finish for me. I think you learned how to do it last night."

Yes, he had. Squeezed the udders till those suckers were dry as bones. And never wanted to put his hand on another goat nipple as long as he lived. "Aren't you almost done?" he asked.

"Still have Ruffles and the little girls. And I need to leave in less than an hour."

He sat up completely. "Where are you going?"

"County Clerk to get to the bottom of this Burns guy and his bogus will."

Except, the will was not bogus. Elliott was certain of that. How Burns's client was able to coerce the old man to sign it might not have been the most ethical of means, but the will was legal. "I'm going with you."

That earned him a vile look. "No, you're staying here to milk the goats."

"I'll do both, but I'm going with you."

"I can handle it. I've already started, to be honest. Last night I Googled that lawyer and the name of his client."

Oh, that was not good. "What did you find?"

"He's a real lawyer, sadly. But Island Management doesn't have a Web site or anything trackable. But I have some contacts in the county government who helped me after Nonno died without a will or a deed to this land."

Brushing some hay out of his hair and off his jeans, he finally got up from the homemade bed, his real estate experience taking over his brain for a moment. "How can he not have a deed to the land?"

"He was a founder of the island, back in the 1940s. A group of people actually settled the island, and were able to claim ownership of land. That's how the lady who owns Casa Blanca got a lot of that land, from her grandparents who were part of the founding group. But there's a deed now, on file, and in eight, no, seven more days, it transfers to my name."

Not if it transferred to another name first. In six days, if all went according to plan. An unwanted pressure of guilt punched hard enough to push him to a stand. "Let me hit the head and I'll finish the goats, shower, and go with you."

Her jaw unhinged.

He ignored it. "C'mon. You know you want company."

Before she could argue, he was crossing the pen and headed for the trailer, blinking into the blinding sunrise, making plans for who to call first and exactly what strings to pull and palms to grease. He *had* to be at those government offices with her.

Her grandfather was a founder of the island.

He silenced the voice in his head with a litany of rationalization. This place was perfect for the stadium, great access, close to a good population base on the other side of the causeway, still small and out of the way enough to be a real tourist draw. Plus, they'd already secured the surrounding properties, and this little plot shouldn't hold them up. The whole plan wouldn't work without a good access road and parking. This was too *easy* to start over.

Fast, easy, simple, lucrative, and...a shitty thing to do to Frankie.

51

Swearing softly, he stepped inside the little mobile home to find the bathroom in the hall. He'd have to go get some things from the resort if he was going through with this plan, but Frankie had thoughtfully laid out an unopened toothbrush package with toothpaste, a washcloth, and something that looked like a bar of soap. It was brown and lumpy and smelled…amazing.

He sniffed again, getting a mix of sweet and peppery smells. When he turned on the water to lather up, the scents got stronger, and the soap slid around in his hands with a buttery, luscious texture.

If she washed in this stuff, then he wanted to…touch her.

Oh, hell, he wanted to anyway.

He stripped his T-shirt off and took a French bath, imagining how good a whole shower would be, except he didn't think he'd fit in that phone booth of a shower. Once he'd dried off and brushed his teeth, he checked outside and, not seeing her, pulled his phone out of his back pocket and called Zeke.

The hello was very sleepy and not real pleased. "What?"

"Did I interrupt the honeymoon?"

He got a low groan. "We're not married…yet."

Geez, the guy fell hard and fast. "We need to talk."

"You didn't close that Cardinale deal yet, Becker?" Zeke was awake now.

"Working on it."

"Call me when it's done. I'm sleeping." A female voice in the background, followed by a soft laugh, told Elliott that his friend wouldn't be going back to sleep anytime soon. Lucky bastard.

"Well, sorry to delay your morning exercise, but you

have to hear me out. I put an offer on the land through a lawyer who appears to have a legitimate claim naming his client as the owner of the land."

"And?"

"Owner's granddaughter is going to fight it, so I have to delay, distract, and divert her for a week while we slip in under the radar and get the land. And, just in case this lawyer's a shyster and he's lying, then I have to work on buying the land directly from her. Either way, I'm going to win." He felt better just saying it out loud. He had a plan and needed to stick to it.

"Hmm. Okay. Sounds…okay."

"Oh, it's more than okay," he said, reassuring himself as much as Zeke.

"Why, is she hot?"

"A ten."

Zeke snorted. "You are the luckiest son of a bitch on earth."

"Says the man who is in the sack with a gorgeous female while I have a goat waiting to be milked."

"What?"

"It's a goat farm," he explained. "The late owner ran a goat farm, and she took over."

"So why doesn't she want to sell?"

"Sentimental value, best I can tell."

"You can outbid that, Becker."

"Yeah, but she doesn't know about my deal with the lawyer, and she doesn't know what we're planning to build." Another one of those little guilt pricks stabbed at his chest, so he paced the trailer. In three steps, he was in a bedroom he knew had to be Frankie's, decorated—if you could actually use that word—with a simple beige comforter and a few pillows, some pictures of the great outdoors on the walls, and a single dresser with a hairbrush, mirror, and two small, framed photographs.

It didn't look like any woman's bedroom where he'd spent time. He was used to counters that looked like the makeup department at Saks and overflowing closets with a zillion pictures of...themselves. This room was as simple as the farmer who lived in it. And all that did was intrigue him more.

"So, what's your plan?" Zeke asked with a yawn.

"I'm going to, um, stick around her farm." He cleared his throat. "And work."

"What?" Zeke barked out a laugh. "You? Work a farm?"

"Yeah." Leaning over the dresser, he squinted at one of the small pictures. But his focus was on the girl in the photo—definitely Frankie, though a good dozen or more years ago, with the gangly body and braces-heavy smile of a preteen. She stood between two people who were undoubtedly her parents, the mix of features easy to discern.

"Then she must be an eleven, not a ten."

"Grow up, Einstein." Hey, was that the Plaza in the background? A limo driver behind them, waiting with an open door, the small family dressed for a special event. Vacation in New York City? The other picture was of an older man, he'd guess the grandfather she called Nonno, leaning against the shelter Elliott had just slept in. A bull of a man, with a shock of white hair and some teeth missing in his broad grin. One hand was on a goat, the giant, gnarled fingers nearly covering the animal's whole head. Next to him, that same little girl, the braces still on.

54

"So, can you make it?" Zeke's question brought Elliott back to the conversation.

"Sorry, make what?"

"Brunch tomorrow at Casa Blanca. Nate's docked his yacht in the harbor, and he's meeting Mandy and me for brunch. Why don't you come over and join us? I mean, if you can get away from the goats." He chuckled, and in the background, his girlfriend was laughing, too.

But Elliott ignored them, looking from one picture to the other, both of which had to have been taken in the same year. With her grandfather, she had hunched shoulders and a shadow of pain around her young eyes.

"We're meeting around noon at the restaurant. Be there, because I have some great news to announce."

Elliott pictured that great news in bed next to Zeke— the woman he'd known from high school and found not so long ago cleaning his villa over at Casa Blanca. "I can only imagine."

"No, you can't," Zeke said, his voice rich with a contentment that Elliott had never heard in Einstein's tone before.

No surprise, really. Zeke had confessed his longing to settle down awhile back, when he and Elliott had become friends. They'd had Yankees season tickets near each other and had then joined the same recreational softball team. But the very idea of settling anywhere with anyone made Elliott's teeth itch.

Zeke covered the phone, muffling his words but not the woman's laugh. Okay, it didn't sound exactly like hell to be that happy, but the same woman forever? That was not easy enough for Elliott Becker. That was downright...difficult.

He signed off the call and picked up the two pictures

again, looking at them side by side, imagining that little—

"Can I help you find something?"

He jerked around, stunned that he hadn't heard her come in. "Just looking at your pictures."

"Also known as invading my privacy." She strode closer and took the photos, placing them exactly where they'd been on the bureau.

"What happened to your parents?" he asked, letting his gaze shift to the other picture.

She swallowed, hard. "9/11." Her words were so gruff, so soft, he almost didn't understand. But then he did. And he felt his own shoulders sink with the truth.

"Both of them?" God, that wasn't fair. So, so not fair.

She blew out the slowest, saddest breath he'd ever heard, closing her eyes. "Both of them." Her voice cracked on the last word, and he couldn't stop himself from reaching to her and pulling her into his arms.

"Frankie, I'm sorry."

She was stiff at first, but then she molded into him with the next sad sigh. "Not as sorry as I am."

Something in his heart just twisted and cracked and fell right open. Easing her down on the bed purely so he could sit and hold her, he stroked her hair off her face and looked into her eyes.

He shouldn't do this. He shouldn't get personal or care. Zeke and Nate wanted this land, and when they wanted something, they got it. She'd just be the collateral damage of their unstoppable success. Well-paid collateral damage.

His job was to figure out how to get this land, not how to understand her heart. That's why they'd sent him.

Still, he couldn't help himself. "Tell me about them," he whispered.

He felt her lean further into him, one step closer to trust he knew in his gut he didn't deserve. Trust he'd be betraying soon. But he held her anyway because there was no way he couldn't. No way.

Chapter Six

Comfort. Sweet, strong, delicious comfort in the form of muscular arms wrapped around her and a bare chest beating with a heart she wanted to rest against. The consolation felt so good and necessary when she let herself slip to that sad place, so Frankie just let herself fall into Elliott's embrace.

"I really don't talk about it, about them." She swallowed against the rock in her throat, sniffing the lingering smell of lavender and sea salt. "You used my goat's milk soap."

"That creamy stuff?"

She nodded and sniffed again. She'd never smelled it on anyone but herself, and on him it was divine. "I made it."

"Nice." She could feel his face move in a smile against her head. "And nice attempt at a subject change. Talk to me, Frankie."

She exhaled, knowing this man well enough to realize he wouldn't let her stand up and go on until he got what he wanted. Inching back, she met his gaze, unashamed of her tears. "My parents are the reason you can't sway me with money. I really do believe it is the root of all and every evil, including the greed that stole their lives."

He narrowed his eyes. "Greed didn't drive jets into the World Trade Center, Frankie."

"No, but greed had my parents insisting on being workaholics, never missing a day, even an hour. Even that day, when..." She fought the lump again, the injustice, the bad timing, the big fat *what if* that had ruled her life for so long after September 11, 2001.

Every time she'd heard a miracle story about someone who hadn't gone to work at the Twin Towers that day, she choked on her own "what ifs."

"What if they'd skipped work that morning to come to the school open house instead, like they promised they would?" she asked, giving voice to a question she'd asked herself a million times. "What if they'd chosen to meet my new teacher like all the other parents? What if they had a story like that...and they'd been saved?"

He stroked her hair, not saying anything or passing judgment on her bitterness.

"They didn't have to be there that day," she whispered. "They were supposed to be at my school, but some big multimillion-dollar client was coming in that afternoon and at the last minute, they bailed on the school meeting." She closed her eyes, remembering that last breakfast, the punch of disappointment because, once again, money trumped everything else. Not even one of them would pick school over a client, so she'd lost them both.

"And they could be alive if they could have been somewhere else, and they would have been if their priorities had been in order."

"Everyone who died could have been somewhere else, Frankie." His voice was as calm and sweet as the fragrant soap he'd washed with, but the words did nothing to help her.

"But they *should* have been somewhere else," she insisted, clinging to the regret and anger that always bubbled under the surface. "I've forgiven them, but…"

"Not if there's a but you haven't."

Well, she'd tried. It had been thirteen years and she wasn't angry at the world anymore. "But I'll never be a fan of anyone who is motivated by the desire to have more. That's what drove my parents—the need for more. More money, more things, more status, more success, more multigazillion-dollar deals." She puffed out a disgusted breath. "They died to have more."

He didn't respond—how could he? He was a *billionaire* who no doubt worshiped at the altar of More Is Never Enough. But his gentle caress on her back felt like that of a kind, caring man, so she tried to forget that he was cut from the same cloth as her money-hungry parents and let him soothe away the old beast of bitter who reared his head more often since Nonno had died. So maybe it wasn't bitterness that had her blue, maybe it was just a far too familiar sense that she had no one.

She closed her eyes and rested on his powerful shoulder, practically purring at how good he felt.

"I came here after it happened," she finally said, not wanting to talk about her parents anymore. They weren't why she wanted to hold on to this land. It was because of her savior, Nonno. "To live with my grandfather."

"Was he your only relative?"

"No, my mother's sister in Long Island also wanted me, but according to my parents' will, I was supposed to live with Nonno. So I left a four-thousand-square-foot apartment on the Upper East Side and a private school, driver, and a life of pure luxury to move to a goat farm in the middle of a swamp island."

It was his turn to back away and look at her incredulously. "That must have been horrible."

She fought a smile. "I loved it."

"Really?"

"Well, not immediately, no. I mean, it was a bit of a culture shock and I was a typical teenage brat full of denial and anger, but Nonno? Boy, he just loved me like I was another one of his darling does. He was just the most amazing, sweet, terrific guy in the whole world. My grandmother had died a few years earlier, and the farm was fading, but only because he needed a second pair of hands and he was too stubborn to ask for help. His middle name was stubborn," she said, trying to make light of the character trait that had nearly cost her that last goodbye. "But once he started teaching me how to do things, I really, really loved the life."

"You lived in this trailer?" he asked.

"Oh, no. We had a little ranch house, but it was messed up badly in a hurricane that hit the island a few years ago. He put this up temporarily."

"I guess it was a great escape from the pain of what you'd gone through in New York," he said.

Everyone thought that, and it made sense. "It didn't seem like that to me at the time. I enjoyed the animals and loved Nonno and he loved me. Completely and wholly and unconditionally. Way more than my parents did, or at least than they acted like they did."

"Like, he went to your teacher conferences instead of working?"

She laughed softly. "Even better. After the first year at Mimosa High, he yanked me out and homeschooled me because the teachers were all 'from hunger,' he used to say."

"He educated you himself?"

She shrugged. "More or less. He certainly taught me how to milk goats and breed them, and how to make soap and cheese, and get a doe ready to give birth. But that's not exactly what qualifies as an education in the state of Florida."

Comfortable now, she tucked her legs under her and shimmied back to look at him. That was no hardship. His dark gaze was right on her, every word hitting his heart, she could tell.

"And that was a problem," she added. "Enough of a problem that my Aunt Jenny swooped down from New York, went to war with the courts, and got me to go live with her in Roslyn Heights, Long Island, also known as living hell for me."

Which was actually the understatement of all time. "My cousins were entitled, obnoxious, partying bitches, and my aunt and uncle were as money-obsessed as my parents. I don't know how I survived there, but I did."

"Then you came back here?" he guessed.

"I went to Florida State and got a degree in animal science and, of course, I stayed with Nonno on every break and in the summer. The more I learned, the more I had ideas for this place. It has so much potential to be a real money-making operation if he had only brought it into the twenty-first century. But Nonno didn't like...the twenty-first century. He had a rotary phone here until the day he died."

"So that's what you want to do now? Make it a twenty-first-century goat farm?"

"No." She pulled her legs up again, wrapping her arms around her jeans, not liking this part of her story any more than the part about her parents. "I made him a promise that I wouldn't and, honestly, I lost interest in high-tech farming."

"Why?"

"After college I...we..." She closed her eyes against the tears that welled. "We had a bad fight about modernizing this place. I'm telling you, there is no creature on earth as pigheaded and close-minded and obstinate as an old Italian man. I wanted to expand and install a whole milking and dairy system, and he just wanted to make soap and cheese and maybe have a little petting farm and retail storefront when he rebuilt the house. I was on fire with youth and ambition, and he was mellow with age and the simple joys in life. We fought pretty badly." She managed a wry smile. "I may have inherited that stubborn streak."

"Ya think?" Laughing softly, he brushed a strand of her hair off her face, the gesture so intimate it sent an unwanted rush through her, but also encouraging, so she kept talking.

"Anyway, after our big argument, I went to DC and got a really important job at the Department of Agriculture and Nonno..." Her voice hitched, and he reached for her hand, swallowing it in his much more sizable ones. "He had a stroke."

"And you weren't here."

She looked at him, touched for some reason that he would understand just how horrible that was. "No, I wasn't. And if I had been..."

"He still would have had a stroke."

She shook her head vehemently. "But I might have gotten him to the hospital sooner or maybe I would have seen an early symptom." Guilt wracked her voice and pinched her heart. "But I was in Washington...and..." She swallowed but forced herself to make the admission. "I was no better than my parents in being somewhere other than where I should have been, chasing success and big dreams and—"

"Big dreams? In the Department of Agriculture?" He couldn't hide the incredulity in his voice.

"I was on a fast track to a directorship," she countered. "But that's all over now, thankfully."

"Because you promised him you'd run the farm the way he wanted you to?"

"I promised him..." She wasn't really sure if he'd heard that promise, so what did it matter? Damn it, her voice truly cracked then.

"Tell me, Frankie." With a little pressure from his hand, it felt natural to let go of her grip on her legs and allow them to drop, removing the protective barrier she'd created as she told her story. Automatically, Elliott took up the space by getting closer.

She closed her eyes and reminded herself that the promise *did* matter. "He was in a coma when I arrived from DC," she whispered, letting herself be transported back to that night. "I sat with him in the ICU and apologized and promised and begged him to stay alive. But he just stayed completely still and asleep."

Elliott stroked her knuckles, as if to gently coax the story out of her.

"One night, after about two weeks, he woke up, and we talked for hours."

Hadn't they?

"What did you talk about?" Elliott asked, leaning forward, fully invested in the story.

"He wanted me to know he'd forgiven me for leaving and he loved me..." She swallowed so her voice didn't hitch, but the way Elliott caressed her hand nearly did her in. "He wanted this farm to be a perfect slice of heaven with a herd sired by the buck he'd brought over from his home country. So I promised him I'd do exactly that, and I also promised him that I would never, ever let this land be owned by anyone who wasn't in the Cardinale family. And I'm keeping those promises." She closed her eyes. "He died...that night. In fact..."

Her voice faded out, a sob threatening. "Shhh. That's all. You don't have to tell me any more."

But she did. He had to know why this mattered so much to her. "I promised him I'd keep the land and do exactly what he'd wanted to do with it. Then I moved in here for what was going to be a week or two while I figured things out and sifted through his belongings and figured out someone to take care of the farm before I went back to DC."

"How were you going to run the farm from DC?"

"I didn't know," she answered honestly. "But I stayed here a week, then two, then three..." She smiled. "Then I quit my job and decided to stay...for a while."

He lifted a brow. "You just quit this job that was on the fast track?"

She shrugged. "I have, you know, some money from my parents, and I never expected to like it so much here. To feel so...at home." Lonely, but at home.

Something flickered in his expression. A little hurt maybe? A little fear? Perhaps he'd just realized how crappy it would be to try to buy her home. He lifted their joined hands to his mouth, breathing a soft kiss on her knuckles. Goose bumps flowered up her arms, and chills trickled down her spine, but she managed to stay still.

A centimeter of space closed between them, but she wasn't sure who leaned closer to whom…it was like a magnetic force pulling them toward each other for a kiss.

His lips were warm, soft, sweet, and Frankie didn't even bother to fight, opening her mouth just enough to taste his tongue and hope that this wasn't fake and neither was this very sweet man.

"Let me go with you today," he said, his voice surprisingly gruff. "You don't want to be alone."

No, she didn't. Not today, and not…tonight. "Yeah, cowboy. You can come."

Morning sun bounced off the massive glass building that took up a city block when Frankie and Elliott reached the entrance to the County Clerk's offices on the mainland. Despite the brightness, Frankie knew a maze of lines and cubicles lay behind those shiny walls, populated by frustrated people and overworked clerks and wrapped in red tape.

If only she could find Liza, the amazing clerk who'd helped her last time.

"I can't believe I have to go in there again," she sighed. The last time, when she confirmed that the property was hers despite the lack of official paperwork, she'd lost nearly six hours in the place.

Elliott kept a light hand on her back and squinted up at the place, and glanced around the campus of Collier County government buildings. "Nice real estate, though."

"Not if you're stuck inside." At least today, she'd have him next to her, and for some reason she didn't want to examine too closely, she was happy about that. Maybe it was his steady presence or close attention, but she liked having him here.

And she'd liked kissing him back home. A lot.

Just as they stepped under the entrance awning, Elliott paused and reached into his pocket, glancing at his cell. "I have to take this call. Why don't you get started without me? Who are you meeting with, so I can find you?"

"Just call me. Take down my cell."

He looked at the phone with a face that said he had no time for that now.

"Okay, best bet would be in Official Land Records," Frankie said. "The lady who helped me last time was Liza..." She dug into her memory for the woman's last name. "Lemanski! Liza Lemanski."

"Got it." He gave her an impulsive kiss on the forehead and stepped away with the phone to his ear. "This is Becker."

Becker. Even the way he said his last name was sexy. He didn't even look back to say goodbye as he walked away, obviously seeking privacy. Trying not to be disappointed—hell, how had she gotten so used to him already?—she went inside to start the long process of waiting in lines, filling out forms, taking a number, and waiting some more.

About fifteen minutes later, Elliott came up behind her in line.

"I have an emergency," he said softly. "It could take an hour or two. You can handle this on your own?"

"Of course I can," she said quickly, fighting irritation that he would even imply she couldn't. Or maybe it was irritation because he kept disappearing. Or these bureaucrats kept giving her a runaround. Truth was, everything had her irritated right then. She closed her eyes. "This is just frustrating."

"I know." He stepped closer and put a gentle hand on her shoulder. "When we're done, we'll stop by my place at the resort and…" He let his voice fade and, damn it all, didn't her imagination and hormones go wild. "Maybe take a walk on the beach. Have a drink. Relax."

And fall into his bed.

She inched back, not sure where the thought came from, but it sure wasn't the first time she'd had it. With a quick and unexpected peck on her lips, he was gone.

She shifted to her other foot and checked her number again, furious at the way he'd left her so electrified. And disappointed to be alone. Why in God's name would his leaving affect her like that? He was a billionaire, for crying out loud, and it was Monday morning. Of course, he had more important things to worry about than her little property problem.

Just like her parents.

She shoved that thought out of her mind, scrunching her eyes shut to mentally erase the words. Over the course of the next two hours, she met with ineffective clerk after ineffective clerk. Keyboards were pounded, file drawers were opened, then she was sent to another department, then another.

It all reminded her so much of her old job that her stomach clenched. She'd never go back to that, never.

She really did just want her farm and her goats and...

Becker's face flashed in her mind. And his body. And the whole cycle of thoughts started all over again.

Finally, she got to Land Records where she was greeted by a familiar face, and the first one smiling all day.

"Liza!" Frankie reached out to shake her hand, not surprised when the other woman added a friendly hug. They'd gotten pretty darn friendly the last time Frankie had been here, and Liza had been an absolute treasure helping her navigate a maze of red tape and brick walls.

"What are you doing back here?" Liza asked, her stunning turquoise-colored eyes dancing with warmth. "The ninety-day wait period hasn't passed yet."

"I know, but I've been informed that someone has tried to file an illegal will in my grandfather's name."

Liza frowned and gestured to the hall. "I've been digging around since I got the message that you were worming your way through the processing system from hell. C'mon, let's go in my office and talk."

In the windowless room, Frankie took the guest chair, remembering the hominess of the little office, despite its lack of windows and abundance of government-issued ugly furniture. Frankie had seen her share of these four walls, but Liza made hers welcoming, with a lamp on the table instead of fluorescent light and a few pictures of a darling little brown-eyed boy she assumed was Liza's son.

"It's very puzzling," Liza finally said as she slipped into her chair behind the desk. "I found that will a few hours ago when I first got the notification from documents pending that you were looking for it."

Frankie shot forward. "And it's fake, right?"

She blew out a breath. "I don't know. It's disappeared right out of the system not twenty minutes ago."

"What?"

"It's the strangest thing," she said, turning to tap on her computer keyboard as if she hoped it might magically appear again. "I wouldn't have even looked, but a notice came that you were in the process office and would eventually make your way here, and, of course, I remembered you and how there was no will and no deed for your No... What did you call him again?"

"Nonno," she supplied. "It's Italian for grandfather."

Liza smiled. "Yes, I liked that and your story about your farm. It sounds so dreamy, you know?"

"It is," Frankie said, understanding the longing to escape bureaucracy. "You should bring your son to my farm sometime. He'd love the goats."

Liza's smile faltered, and her gaze shifted to the framed picture next to her computer. "Oh, he's not my..." Liza gave a tight smile. "Sure. I'd love to bring him over, thank you." A box flashed on the screen, taking her attention back to the computer. "Ugh, still says 'file not found,' but..."

"But what?" Frankie leaned forward, trying to get a better look at the screen.

"Well, when I saw that notice that you were trying to track down a will and I found it, I had a chance to see the document scan." Her pretty mouth drew down. "I hate to tell you, it looked legit."

"It did?" Worry clamped her chest.

Liza's gaze softened and grew sympathetic, like a doctor about to deliver very bad news. "Frankie, we do see this kind of thing from time to time."

"What kind of thing?"

"Older folks do get scammed like that. These con artists and developers comb old-age homes and even some neighborhoods looking for elderly citizens who haven't written a will, then they persuade the person, who is oftentimes not completely, you know…" She tapped her temple and gave a sympathetic tilt to her head.

"Nonno was pretty alert," Frankie said. But then, she'd been gone awhile. How did she know how alert he was? She didn't know he was sick enough to have a stroke, either.

"I'm sure he was, but in some cases, these people don't know what they're signing because they don't have family to advise them."

And neither had Nonno, because she was in Washington, DC. Tamping down guilt, she leaned forward. "Can you fight that?"

"Oh, absolutely, with the right attorney. Unless, of course, the land gets sold before you get a hold of it. Then you're in trouble."

Frankie pinched the bridge of her nose, squeezing against the frustration headache that had started hours earlier. "So, what happened to the document?"

Liza whooshed out a breath that fluttered her bangs. "I do not know, and I tell you, I'm freaking Sherlock Holmes when it comes to investigating things like this. I've dug through every file I can find, but it's gone."

"Then, that's good, right?"

She shook her head. "It's just weird. It could mean that it was flagged by someone, somewhere, and pulled from the system, or it could mean that someone made an offer on the land and a Realtor has the will."

Frankie sucked in a breath. "No!"

"Don't panic yet. I'm going to make this a top priority, and I promise to call you when I find it. Is this still your cell number?" She read from the open file, and Frankie confirmed.

Liza walked out with her, still chatting as they went down the hall, but when she opened the door, she went stone silent. Then she turned to Frankie. "Brace yourself. Hottie in the office."

Frankie laughed, remembering how a handsome man could send a reaction fluttering through the otherwise dull halls of a government building. She inched around to take a peek, her whole body tightening at what she saw. Not a hottie...*her* hottie.

"There you are," Elliott said, coming toward her with outstretched hands. "I thought you got lost in the maze."

Instead, she was lost in an unexpected embrace.

She turned to say goodbye to Liza, who was staring hard at Elliott, a frown tugging as if she was trying to place him.

"Liza, this is Elliott Becker. Elliott, Liza Lemanski, the most helpful person in this building."

Elliott nodded hello. "Helpful, as in you straightened everything out?"

"Not exactly," Frankie said. "But thanks for trying, Liza."

She gave a wave, and another scrutinizing look at Elliott, which Frankie imagined he was used to, though Liza wasn't exactly salivating; she was more curious than anything. "Nice to meet, you Elliott Becker." She said his name slowly, as if trying to place it or remember it for later.

With a final nod, he gave Frankie a nudge forward. "Let's go celebrate."

She eyed him. "Celebrate what? The brick wall I just ran into?"

He shrugged quickly. "Well, my business situation went well."

"I guess one of us should be happy." The weird thing was, despite the frustrations of the last few hours, she felt oddly happy right here on his arm.

That was weird, wasn't it?

Chapter Seven

"I don't believe it." Frankie stood with her hands perched on her hips, turning once to survey the plush, high-end villa, called Rockrose. Tucked into a garden and looking out over the aquamarine waters and pure white sands of Barefoot Bay, this one-bedroom vacation home was private, expensive, and perfectly appointed.

"You don't believe what?" Elliott asked as he joined her.

"That you would willingly choose to sleep on hay in a goat shelter when you are paying God knows what for this place."

He laughed. "I told you I'm eccentric."

"Or nuts."

"A little of both. Wait here, I'm going to get some stuff." He headed to the back, presumably the bedroom, giving her a moment to inspect the luxurious furnishings and finishings. Light, tropical fabrics accented the dramatic Moroccan-style architecture of the whole resort, with rich wood floors leading to a pool and patio. But it was the front veranda and the water view that captivated Frankie, so she stepped back outside to lean against the rail and drink in nature's finest work.

At the sound of male laughter on the beach, she spotted two men, both tall and shirtless, talking as they walked up the beach, straight toward the villa. Speaking of nature's finest work. Both great-looking, both built to break hearts, they got closer and Frankie couldn't decide which one was easier on the eyes.

Might have been a tie.

She zeroed in on the man on the left, his chestnut hair and square jaw so familiar, she couldn't resist squinting to get a better look. He laughed and made a gesture, and even that seemed like something she'd seen before.

They glanced at the villa then, and both men slowed their steps as they noticed her.

"Holy shit," she whispered, recognizing the man on the left. "That's Nathaniel Ivory."

Behind her, Elliott stepped onto the veranda. "Holy shit is right. What the hell do they want?"

"You know him?" She wanted to turn to see Elliott's face, but didn't want to miss a minute of "Naughty Nate." Shirtless, no less.

"Yeah, I know him."

"Dang, I left my phone in the car. I want to get a picture."

He choked softly. "To sell to the tabloids for fifty grand? Thought you didn't care about money, Frankie."

"Who said anything about selling it?" she teased.

He was next to her in an instant, but both men lifted their hands in greeting.

"Nice of you to show up, Becker," Nate called.

"You really *do* know him." She couldn't keep the awe out of her voice, which earned her a dark look.

"He's not your type."

She bit back a smile and looked at Nate again. "Oh, honey, Naughty Nate is everyone's type."

He mumbled a curse and practically leapt off the veranda, heading them off as they came closer.

"I want to meet him," she called playfully.

Elliott purposely ignored that, and Frankie didn't know what gave her more of a secret thrill—that he was jealous or that she was about to meet the equivalent of American royalty. The Ivory name was synonymous with power, money, and juicy scandals. With hands in every business and half of Hollywood and a lot of Congress, there was an Ivory on the front page of the news regularly.

Out of earshot, the three of them talked for a minute, then Nate and the other man gave her friendly waves. Frankie took that as an invitation and joined them on the paved path that separated the house from the beach.

"These are some friends of mine, Frankie," Elliott said, gesturing to the men. "Zeke Nicholas and Nate Ivory."

She looked from one to the other while she shook hands, politely not ogling their chests, but still stealing a few peeks.

"So this is who has Becker's full attention this week," Nate said, giving her a world-famous once-over that had made millions of women swoon. Oddly, it had no effect, but that might have been because Becker held his own with these two men.

"It seems he has a strange desire to be around goats," she told them.

Both men could barely hide their amusement. "I think

76

it has a lot more to do with the goatherd than the herd of goats," Zeke said, grinning at her.

The statement did crazy things to her insides, far more than Nate Ivory's flirtatious wink that said he agreed.

"So, what brings you here?" she asked.

"It's a…baseball thing," Nate said.

"Softball, actually," Elliott corrected him. "We're all on the same softball team."

"Really?" Well, it certainly made sense that they were athletes with those bodies. "That must be fun to watch." For any female with a pulse. "Are you planning to play while you're all here? I'd love to see a game."

"No," Elliott said quickly. "We're not, we're—"

"Bad," Zeke added. "Not pretty to watch."

She smiled up at him. "I doubt that."

"What are you two talking about?" Nate asked. "The Niners are fantastic to watch."

"The Niners? That's your team?" Frankie shifted her gaze to Becker, who looked more than a little uncomfortable. Was he jealous of these guys? That seemed a little preposterous, but something was bugging him.

"Yeah," Zeke answered. "The Niners."

"What does the name mean?" Frankie asked.

They all shared a look and a silent communication that she couldn't decipher.

"It means…" Nate dragged out the words.

"Nine on a team?" she guessed.

"Zeroes," Becker finally said. "Net worth."

It took a few seconds for that to register, then she understood those nine zeroes meant a billion. "All of you?"

"More or less," Elliott said. "So now I'm sure you don't want to see us play."

Because she'd made her feelings about billionaires clear enough to him. She gave an easy shrug. "Might still be fun."

Elliott put a hand on her shoulder and started to steer her away. "Great to see you guys. I'll try and catch lunch in the next couple of days, but I'm really busy."

"On the farm," Nate said, fighting amusement.

"With the goats," Zeke added, equally entertained by the thought.

"And the goatherd who is obviously a helluva lot better looking than you two clowns." He whisked her away, calling over his shoulder, "We'll be in my villa. Read the sign: Do not disturb."

He sure seemed anxious to get her away from them. Or at least...alone in the villa.

Elliott wasted little time throwing the rest of what he needed in his bag, making sure Zeke and Nate were gone. He'd warned them off any mention of the baseball stadium, but the chance of letting something slip worried him. Plus, witnessing Nate flirt with Frankie irked the crap out of him.

She was...his. At the moment, anyway.

"This place is really amazing," she said as he came out of the bedroom with his bag.

"As you said, it beats the double-wide." He gave her a wink. "Anytime you want to move over here, I'm game."

She angled her head and gave him a *get real* look. "I'd like to see more of the resort, though. Especially because I have a meeting with the spa manager this week. Can you give me a tour?"

He'd risk running into Nate and Zeke again, but it beat goat work. "Sure."

An hour later, Elliott snagged a picnic lunch from the restaurant and persuaded Frankie to walk to the nearby harbor, where they settled on a wide, whitewashed dock to enjoy the afternoon sunshine. It was warm enough that Frankie slipped off the sweater she wore over a strapless sundress, revealing shapely bare shoulders and a surprising sneak peek of cleavage.

He couldn't help admiring the lovely picture she made as she leaned back on her hands and lifted her face to the sun which, despite being February, was quite warm.

"Your friends are funny," she said. "And that Nate is as good in three dimensions as he looks on the covers of tabloids in two."

He faked a choke. "And here I thought you were different from most women."

"I am," she insisted, taking the cold shrimp he offered. "But I'm still human."

He looked skyward. "Change the subject."

"Deal. What do you want to talk about?"

Her land. Besides a deathbed promise, what else was he taking from her? The question had plagued him, and it felt like the right time to ask. "So what exactly are your plans for your grandfather's farm?"

"It's my farm now," she said quickly. "And my plan is to fulfill the vision he'd always had. La Dolce Vita."

"The Sweet Life." He'd heard the expression.

"That's what Nonno called it. He didn't want to turn it into some big high-tech farm, but he always wanted to see it be a little country store and destination for families. Before Casa Blanca was built, not enough people came to Barefoot Bay to make that a reality, which is part of the reason I fought him on it and wanted to go in a different direction. But now I see the wisdom of his ways, and that's exactly what I'm going to do."

Except, she wouldn't if La Dolce Vita was transformed into an access road and stadium parking. He swallowed, but the bite lodged in his throat, making him down half a bottle of water while she stared out at the horizon, deep in thought.

"Don't you feel you're making his dreams come true and not yours?" he asked.

She considered that, then shook her head. "I've wrestled with what to do, but the more I'm there, the more it feels right. I think I'll build a cute two-story house made of stone like the ones in Italy. I'll live upstairs, but downstairs would be the retail shop. Something small, you know? I would sell my soaps and milk and cute little goat-related products. I'd have a petting pen and a much nicer milking shed and production area."

Whoa, these plans were a little further along than he'd realized. "Sounds like you might need some cash to make all that happen." With cash from the sale of her land, could she build her farm somewhere else? Would that assuage his guilt?

She shrugged. "I told you, I have some money tucked away."

"But do you have millions?"

She turned from the water to stare hard at him. "You're still convinced you can buy me."

"Not you," he corrected. "But your land."

"I haven't dissuaded you from your eccentric farm dreams yet?"

"Absolutely not. And if you had a lot of money, you could make that dream bigger, better, even more beautiful"—he took a breath and leaned closer— "somewhere else."

"So could you," she replied. "Why my land?"

Because it was next to the other three plots they'd already secured. Because this location was perfect. Because it was easy, and Elliott liked things to be easy.

Except...he also liked them to be fair.

"Anyway," she said, unaware of the war of words raging in his head. "Until I settle that issue with the lawyer who claims someone else owns the land, I couldn't sell it if I wanted to. Second, I don't want to. And I don't care if you call me stubborn, since I told you I come by that trait honestly."

He shook his head, recognizing the impact of a brick wall when he hit it.

He reached for a stray hair and brushed it off her face, studying her strong profile, the little bump on her nose and the thick lashes that brushed her cheek when her eyes were closed. "You're pretty when you're stubborn."

She tilted her head to rest against his hand. "Now you're just trying to play me."

He threaded some hair through his fingers and added a little pressure so she would turn to face him. "I swear I'm not doing anything but sitting in the sunshine with a gorgeous woman, enjoying food and conversation, and thinking about how much I want to kiss her."

With a sigh, she scooted around to face him with her whole body, crossing her legs under her flouncy skirt and forcing him to make eye contact. "I never know when you're being real."

"I'm always..." But was he? "I'm being totally real about wanting to kiss you."

She shook her head, helping herself to a chocolate-covered strawberry, nibbling while she scrutinized him. "I think I know what bothers me most about you, Becker." She pointed the bitten end at him.

He had to laugh. "Now there's a loaded statement. Sounds like the whole 'bother' list is pretty damn long."

"Endless," she agreed with a wry smile. "But this is the big one: Sometimes you're Texan, sometimes you're not. Sometimes you're cocky, sometimes you're sweet. Sometimes you play a little slow on the uptake, sometimes your smarts are daunting. Sometimes you say you're on my side, sometimes you're clearly on the other team."

For a long time, he said nothing, debating all of the different possible responses to that, and not liking any of them.

"And sometimes..." A slow smile curved her lips and her eyes sparkled as she flipped the strawberry stem on a paper plate. "I really like you and, yeah, sometimes I want to kiss you, too."

"I don't want to hear about the other times," he said softly, meeting her almost halfway. "Let me know which Becker you like, and that's the one I'll be."

She popped back. "See? That's what I don't like. The

ability to change and shift and transform to suit the moment. You do that, you know."

Why lie? "I know. I like things to be expedient. So I've learned to, I don't know..." He dug around for the least offensive way to describe himself. "I've learned to blend in with whoever I'm around," he finally said.

She curled her lip like her last bite had been bad. "Don't you want to fix that trait?"

"I'm not quite thirty yet," he said. "I will, in time."

"Then call me when you do, Becker." She reached out and trailed a featherlight touch on his cheek. "If it's the guy I like, I might be up for some of that kissing you mentioned. If it's the phony guy who says what he thinks he needs to say to get what he wants, I'm out."

He snagged her wrist before she could pull her hand away, wrapping his fingers around the narrow bones. "I want to be the Becker you like," he said gruffly.

"Just be the only Becker there is. I mean, how can you be anyone else?"

He rubbed his hand up and down her arm, then let their fingers entwine as he managed to get a little closer. "I moved a lot as a kid."

She regarded him, silent, waiting for whatever that had to do with his ever-changing personality. A lot, he knew.

"I developed an incredible ability to fit in, no matter where I was. Vermont, Texas, Carolinas, big city, small town, on the base or off, every year or so I was in a completely new environment, and I knew survival depended on fitting in."

"Lousy excuse for being a phony," she shot back, the utter lack of sympathy causing a ping inside but not really surprising him.

"I'm not phony," he insisted. "I prefer to think of myself as a chameleon."

She rolled her eyes. "Semantics. Fake is fake."

"I'm not fake. I don't see what's wrong with bending with the wind a little if it makes other people happy and moves things along smoothly. When I'm hanging with my softball team, I'm one of the masters of the universe with nine zeroes. When I'm doing a deal, I'm a commercial real estate mogul. When I'm home with my folks, I'm their ordinary son."

"Who are you right now?"

He smiled and opened his mouth, but she put her fingers over his lips. "The honest truth, Becker. No jokes, no saying what you think I want to hear. Right now, who are you?"

"A guy who really, *really* wants to kiss you." He leaned closer. "Honest, unwashed truth."

She shook her head. "And you're also that real estate mogul who wants to buy my property."

He gave a shrug, not denying that. "He wants to kiss you, too." He closed the rest of the space between them. "A lot."

He expected her to dodge him, but she stayed perfectly still, letting him place his lips on hers for a slow, tender kiss. A strawberry and chocolate kiss, as warm as the tropical sun and light as the bay breeze that lifted her hair and ruffled her skirt.

With a barely audible moan, she tilted her head and let him intensify the contact, their clasped hands separating so they could add light touches. He caressed her bare shoulder, and she tunneled her fingers into his hair.

"I like *this* Elliott," she whispered into the kiss. "But I don't know when you'll change."

As much as he didn't want to, he leaned back, far enough to allow their eyes to focus. "I don't change. I adapt to a situation. It's me, all the time, but I won't deny I know how to work people to get what I want. Is that so bad?"

She smiled, shaking her head. "Only to the people who are being manipulated by you—and I have a feeling I'm one of them right now."

"You call it *manipulated,* but I call it really nice and natural kissing." He underscored that with a longer, deeper kiss, teasing her lips and teeth with his tongue, enjoying a pure rush of pleasure through his body. His hand slid into her hair, easing her even closer. "God, you smell pretty and taste good."

She let out a little sigh as he dragged his lips across her cheek and along her jaw. "You smell like that soap I used in the bathroom," he murmured.

"I made that."

"Mmm. Nice work."

Her throat caught, making him want to explore that skin with his lips, too, but she backed away. "And speaking of soap, if I don't stop making out and start making soap, I won't have a batch ready for that meeting with Jocelyn Palmer. So..." She was trying to push away, but he did his best to hold her in place.

"Am I really going to lose to goat soap?" he asked.

"Goat's *milk* soap," she corrected. "And, yes, I need to get back to work."

He let her stand, easily rising with her. "I can help."

"But..." She hesitated as he got closer, looking up at him as he loomed taller. "There's nothing for you to do. It's a one-person job."

"Then I'll watch and inspire."

She made a face of pure disgust. "How on earth am I going to get rid of you? Don't you have something else to do? Sell buildings? Count your money? Play with your Niners?"

He shook his head, slipping his arm around her. "Nope. You're all I've got this week."

"Lucky me." She snorted with derision, but he could tell she didn't mean it, not the way she was looking at him. "I wish you *were* real, Elliott Becker. You're funny and great-looking and kiss like a dream."

"I *am* real. What do I have to do to prove that to you?"

She pressed a little more into him, her curves fitting nicely against him, her upturned face as beautiful as any view around him. "Kiss me again."

"With pleasure." Lowering his head, he tightened his embrace and kissed her mouth, lifting her up to her tiptoes and into his body. This time he didn't let go, opening his lips and letting their tongues curl and collide, dragging his hand down her spine to settle low on her back and press a little more.

She let out a tiny moan of pleasure, and her fingers tightened on his arms. Both of their hips rocked imperceptibly toward each other in a natural, ancient, raw movement that neither one could have stopped if they'd wanted to.

Blood thrummed from his head to his lower half, and her body shuddered at the first pressure of his.

Finally, before he grew so hard he couldn't hide it, he let her go.

"How'd that feel, goat girl?"

"Real."

He gave a smug smile and took her home.

Chapter Eight

On any other day, Frankie found the process of making soap from her goat's milk relaxing and pleasurable. Today, with Elliott right behind her, glued like a shadow, taking every chance to touch or bump or make body contact, she was anything but relaxed. Each touch was electrifying.

Ozzie circled Elliott's feet, staying as close as possible while the goats positioned themselves around the kitchen area of the milking shed, mostly content to watch. Not Elliott. He wanted to be right on her heels—or ass, to be more precise—nosing over her shoulder, asking clueless questions, making her...jittery.

He practically kissed her ear as he leaned over her to watch her stir the lye into the mixture.

"Back away or you'll get burned," she warned.

But of course he didn't. "Is that stuff making the soap hot?"

"Kind of." Like he was doing to her. Ugh. She had to give him something to do or she'd melt like the waxy soap ball. "What are you good at, Elliott?"

"Besides everything?"

She laughed. "In the soap-making department."

"Whatever you need me to do, I'm good at it."

She had to smile at his infectious confidence, inexplicably attracted to it. "You're probably pretty good at marketing. I need to come up with some catchy names for my fragrances. See that row of bottles?" She indicated the shelf stocked with tiny vials of essential oils she used in the soaps. Go smell them and tell me what they make you think of."

"Okay. Do you have a certain theme you're looking for?"

"Something that would capture the essence of this island, I think. Something that has a local flair, so it would be tropical and beachy and sunwashed."

"Sunwashed?" He gave a soft laugh as he unscrewed one vial and sniffed. "Whoa. Too strong for sunwashing."

"Well, I dilute them, and be careful, some of them are super potent. It's best to put a tiny dab on a cotton ball and sniff that."

After a second, she heard him inhale deeply. "Oh, that's nice. Smells like a really sultry woman. Someone who likes to…"

She cringed, not knowing what to expect.

"Milk goats." He was close to her again, so close she startled, almost dropping the spatula. Without warning, he lifted her hair, exposing her neck. She'd changed into jeans and a tank top, covered with an apron and was currently up to her elbows in rubber gloves and lye… but he made her feel naked.

"What are you doing?"

"Testing the fragrance. I need to smell it on you."

Soft cotton tickled her skin, followed by a warm breath. "Mmm. Almond?"

"Yes." The scent was strong and distinctive, but her whole body was reacting to touch, not smell. Tingling, tightening, bracing for a man.

"It gave you goose bumps," he observed, kissing a few and making the chills worse.

"Now there's a fragrance name. Goose bumps."

He chuckled into another light kiss, disguised as a sniff.

"That won't sell." He kissed her skin again. "You know what gave me goose bumps?"

She wasn't sure she wanted to hear, but waited while he stroked her shoulder.

"The first time I saw you at the resort." He rubbed a slow, small circle. "Running away from me with your hair flying and your cute little bare feet in the sand."

She stood stone still, not caring that the soap might gel if she didn't stir fast enough. She had to hear the rest.

"When you turned around, with the sun setting like back lighting on you, it gave me chills." He kissed the spot he'd been rubbing, pressing his lips to her skin until it burned. "So let's call this one…Casa Blanca Sunset."

She couldn't help sucking in a surprised breath. "That's so pretty!"

"Exactly what I thought when I saw you."

Laughing, she tilted her face toward him. "You really are good. Gifted, in fact."

He let their foreheads touch. "One down. How many do I need to name again?"

"As many as you can, but I'd like four." If she could take it.

Another kiss, and he was gone, opening more bottles and sniffing. She busied herself by pouring out some of the mixture and finding her emulsifier to make the froth that would give the soap its creamy texture.

"This is nice." He inhaled loudly. "What's a mimosa flower?"

"It's why the island you're on is called Mimosa Key. They're incredibly bright pink, fuzzy flowers that bloom everywhere in the spring."

"Sounds like a drink to me. Do you have anything that smells like an orange?"

"Extract. There should be some over there." She touched the button of the electric emulsifier, the low hum drowning out other sounds and sending a slight vibration up her hand as she worked the liquid into a froth.

Suddenly, his hand was over hers, gripping the tool with her, his other hand under her nose with a cotton ball. "What's that smell like?"

Tangy oranges and sweet flowers. Maybe... "Brunch on the Beach?"

"Yeah, but let's go with something more poetic. Mimosa Mornings."

"Oh." She dropped her head back, letting it hit his solid shoulder. "You're a genius."

He dragged a finger over her lips, her chin, and her throat. "You inspire me."

She kept her eyes closed, flicking off the emulsifier to revel in a different buzz, the slight touch of his fingertip on her breastbone.

"Let me put it right here and see how it smells." Turning her to face him, he held her gaze for one second, then dipped his head, past her mouth, lower, lower to brush his mouth right along the top of her protective apron. His tongue flicked in her cleavage.

"Um, Becker. People aren't going to eat my soap."

He chuckled and slowly lifted his head. "When a woman smells this good, I want a taste."

The aroma wafted up, as sweet and light as the kiss on her lips. He kept it chaste and quick, leaving her wanting more when he stepped away. "We've got morning and sunset covered. Let me see what I can cook up for nighttime."

That she knew she couldn't take. "That's probably enough."

He inched back. "Don't you want four?"

"I want..." She let out a nervous laugh. "To stop giving you excuses to kiss me."

His eyes gleamed with satisfaction. "Be right back."

When he stepped away, she finished creaming the mixture and catching her breath, not daring to look over her shoulder at him. Maybe she should find a reason to go into the trailer, lock the door, and wait him out. Maybe she should—

"Night-Blooming Jasmine," he said. "I like the sound of that."

"It's—"

"Seductive."

She smiled and slipped off her latex gloves, stepping away from the soap mixture to get her molds. As she turned, he was right there, inches away.

"Close your eyes," he ordered.

"I don't need to."

"Close and enjoy this."

Enjoy what? Another trip down to her breasts? What did he have in mind now? "Elliott..."

He lifted a cotton ball to her nose, his expression disappointment. "I really like this one, but I want you to close your eyes so you can really appreciate this scent."

She inhaled, a zing going to every pleasure center in her body. "Oh, what is that?"

"Chamomile and lavender."

She took another whiff. "What do you call it?"

"I call it..." He hesitated a few beats, making her look at him.

"You have no idea, do you?"

"Barefoot at Twilight," he finally said.

She let out a soft gasp at the perfect name, and he caught the inhale in a kiss, wrapping his arms around her to pull her into him. "You like it?"

Really, what wasn't to like? "I think that Jocelyn will love these fragrances and this whole concept and then she will buy tons of my soap, ensuring that I have every reason to stay right here on my goat farm where I belong, which..." She inched back and winked at him. "Makes me wonder if you really know what you're doing."

He didn't smile but looked at her for a long time. "Makes me wonder, too," he said, his voice hoarse. Suddenly, he let her go. "So, we've got one more. We have morning, sunset, and twilight. What's left?"

"Midnight."

"I'm thinking something tropical, like that coconut—" He froze, eyes wide. "Did you hear someone scream?"

"Oh, that was Dominic." She was so used to the bays and bleats, she barely heard her buck calling. "He's..." She laughed. "He's kind of frustrated and...you know. Worked up."

"Must be something in the water around—"

The goat cry was louder now and followed by the metallic smack of his pen gate hitting the fence.

"I think he got out!" Frankie whipped around to

run to the shelter door. Not good. This was not good.

Elliott was on her heels, and they both rushed outside at the same time, to find Dominic charging straight toward them, wailing in fury and excitement at his freedom.

"Holy shit, he's mad," Frankie said. "He could bust right into this pen."

"He won't." Elliott tore to the gate and leaped over it again, going straight for the buck, who hesitated and stumbled in surprise. "Whoa, slow down there, big boy."

He was a big boy, too. A Salerno goat the size of a small pony, with a shiny red and black coat and powerful twisted horns, Dominic was everything one expected from an Italian boy.

"Careful," she called. "He has a temper. And he's obstinate. And can be a little stupid when he's this horny."

Elliott grinned, slowly approaching the goat, holding out his hands. "Easy, boy. None of the girls in the goat pen are interested in hotheaded, stupid, stubborn guys."

But behind her, Agnes and Lucretia bayed and danced, as though they could contradict that statement. They were always ready for a party, and that just made Dominic throw his head back and howl.

"Damn, he's ready to rock and roll," Elliott said, taking a step closer.

Just then, Dominic whipped around, his full focus on Elliott. He lowered his head and charged, head-butting Elliott right onto his ass.

Frankie slammed her hand over her mouth, not sure if she should laugh or go try to save him, but Elliott rolled and got up so fast she didn't have a chance to do anything.

"I don't think so, goat boy," Elliott muttered, his muscles tense, his backside dusty. He took a few more slow steps, jumping to the side to miss another butt. "We're done here, Dominic."

"We have to get him back into his pen," Frankie said. "I don't know how to do that, either, because he's never escaped since I've been here."

"Let's go, Dominic." Elliott carefully approached him and got his hand on the goat's neck. "Let's go—"

Dominic whipped from side to side, butting hard again, but this time Elliott held his balance and managed to get his arms around the goat's neck.

All the does were out of the shelter now, screaming and scuffing their hooves, the acrid smell of the buck as exciting as the fight. Frankie held two of them back, walking closer to the fence, mesmerized as Elliott tried to lead Dominic back to his pen.

Dominic bucked again, snapping with open teeth at Elliott's arm.

"Shit, he bites!"

No kidding. Frankie nodded, half-laughing, half-holding back a moan. Dom bit, kicked, and head-butted when he was content, for crying out loud, and right now he was one pissed-off buck.

"Come on, boy, come on." Elliott braved another bite, swearing furiously as he worked to keep his balance and move the buck away. "You gotta go back home."

As if he understood, Dominic jerked out of Elliott's grip again and started to run in the direction of the road.

"Sonofabitch!" Elliott took off after him, a few feet behind, both running full force with dirt and stones flying.

Elliott grabbed hold of him, practically wrestling the

goat to a stop, getting yet another buck and bite in the process. But Elliott held on tight, his legs wide, his powerful arms finally, finally subduing the goat.

"We're going home," Elliott said through gritted teeth, clearly in control now. "Move it!"

Like a chastised puppy, Dominic gave up the fight and plodded back around the trailer to his pen, each step more humble than the one before. Elliott, on the other hand, looked downright victorious.

And sexy as sin.

Frankie didn't even hesitate, leaving the does in their pen and rushing to join Elliott at Dominic's enclosure. Battling for breath, his face red, two bites swelling on his arms, Elliott led Dominic into his pen, standing over him just to let the poor buck know exactly who was in charge. Frankie stayed on the outside to right the latch, watching with a pounding heart and soaring affection.

Finally, Elliott patted the buck and led him to the water bowl. "That's enough of that shit, Dom." Wiping his face with a dirty arm, he ambled out of the pen and double-checked the lock.

"Elliott." Frankie was almost as breathless as he was. "That was—"

She threw her arms around him and kissed him so hard she knocked him right back on his ass.

High on the fight, humming with a surge of adrenaline, and inhaling a heady mix of pretty perfumes and disgusting goat, Elliott took Frankie's kiss and gave it right back to her. He rolled her over on the grass, getting right on top of her to savor his win and this woman. She clutched his head, then his shoulders, almost as if she wanted to stop what she'd started, then wrapped her arms around his whole body and gave in.

Pressing her into the grass, he kissed her mouth, their tongues instantly tangling, their bodies rocking against each other like they'd been waiting all day to do that.

He had, that was certain, and it sure felt like she had, too.

Elliott gave in to the urge to explore whatever inch of her body his hand could find. Face, neck, shoulders, then he slide lower to her breast, making her hiss in a breath when he brushed over her nipple.

"Looks like more than one gate broke around here, Frankie," he teased between kisses.

"I just wanted to…thank you." She was fighting for control, he could tell. And every time he touched or kissed her, she lost a little more of the fight.

They rolled again, and this time he pulled her on top, loving the pressure of her body on his, already responding with blood rushing to harden him. Her eyes widened as she felt that between her legs.

"You know," he whispered with a sly smile. "We can't let poor Dominic see this. He'll go nuts." Laughing, he pushed her up and brought them both to a stand, kissing her again and walking her away from the pens, around the trailer, to the shade of a massive oak tree.

Still joined at the mouth and hip and hands, he leaned her against the tree trunk and pushed his entire body against hers as they kissed. His fingers found the apron tie in the back, snapping the string so he could get one less layer of material between his body and hers.

But it was stuck around her neck. "Take this off," he ordered.

"Becker..."

"Not everything, just the apron. I have a no-apron make-out policy."

She put both hands on his shoulders and inched him back. "You have two buck bites on your arms, your face is bleeding, and my guess is this"—she gave a gentle squeeze to his ribs, making him grunt in pain—"hurts like a mother."

Still cringing, he nodded. "But, so does"—he rocked his lower half into her, biting his lip to hold back a groan of pain and pleasure—"this."

She searched his face, desire crashing with common sense in her golden-brown eyes. "I should take care of your other injuries...first."

"First." His smile tipped up. "That's encouraging."

"Becker, come on. I barely know you."

He slid his hand up her arm, lingering over her shoulder, tempted to take it south and torture her by touching her breasts again, but he dragged his palm in the opposite direction to cup her jaw. "What better way to get to know me?"

"Oh, I can think of several. Talking. Exchanging information. Watching you to see what kind of man you are."

"I'm a buck-saving, goat-toe-clipping, soap-naming, hay-baling assistant goatherd."

She laughed. "Well, when you put it that way, what more could I want?"

"Exactly." He smothered her neck with kisses again,

licking her lightly until he got to her mouth, where he gave it full force. She stiffened and melted and moaned, meeting each sweet press of his lips with one of her own.

"Becker…" She gave his bruised ribs another squeeze. Hard.

"Yeow!"

"Let's get you cleaned up and in a shower." She reached up and kissed his cheek, stinging the spot where he knew a goose egg was growing under his eye. "A cold one."

She should have said *freezing*, because fifteen minutes later, he was stuffed into a Hobbit-sized shower under biting cold spray. But after having Frankie's tender hands all over him with antiseptics and wet cloths, he needed a cold dousing.

Facing the stream of water, he closed his eyes and ignored the sting on his cheek where he'd come in direct contact with a goat horn.

He breathed carefully, since every deep inhale hurt his ribs. But the pain wasn't what shot fire through him. It was the memory of Frankie under him, the hunger in her kiss, the smell and taste and rawness of their connection, which was so real.

She might think he was a fake, but this attraction was genuine. He glanced down at his growing erection. Didn't that prove it?

He leaned against the plastic wall, slightly out of the stream of water, automatically fisting himself and thinking about the way her breast had felt in his hand. The first stroke just made his stomach drop, so he let go, blinking water out of his eyes to find some soap.

Not seeing any, he took a steadying breath and put his face under the water, unable to resist the burning need to touch himself again. To imagine her slender, feminine hands stroking him just...like...that.

"You need soap?"

His eyes popped open at the sound of Frankie's voice on the other side of a flimsy white shower curtain.

"Yeah." His response came out gruff as he flattened his hands on the wall to keep them off his dick as the water picked up temperature. "Bet you have plenty of that, huh?"

"And none of it has a name yet." Her hand reached in, holding one of her brown and yellow bars of goat's milk soap. "I call this one...Morning Shower."

Reaching for the soap, he captured her hand, too, giving it a slight tug. "Man, do you lack imagination."

She laughed and slipped out of his grip. "That's why I need you."

He took the soap and sniffed. "Spicy," he said.

"Yes! There's sage in there." She was so close, just one thin piece of plastic away. All he had to do was slide that curtain and...

Instead, he rolled the soap in his hand, foaming up. "Nice lather."

"That's not a very good name."

Laughing, he gently soaped his ribs. "Shit, that hurts."

"I'm afraid 'shit that hurts' won't sell, either." The curtain moved slightly, and he waited, not breathing, but she didn't draw it back. "I was thinking about something a little more, you know...sexy. Got anything?"

Right here, sweetheart. He stroked himself, once, quickly, closing his eyes as the suds intensified the pleasure against his insanely sensitive skin. "I might be able to come...up with something."

He heard her throat catch with a laugh. "You know what I mean. Does that scent make you think of anything…evocative?"

Like her mouth when she opened it to his or the sweet curve of her ass when she bent over to pick up a milk bucket? That was *evocative* as hell.

With his palms covered with lather, he tried to wash his body, but his hands just went right back to the place where he wanted her fingers to be. Sliding up and down, fondling his tingling balls, rounding the tip with her—

"Got anything?" she asked.

Other than a raging boner? "Um…let's see. I'm thinking about…" *Sliding. Into.* "You."

She chuckled. "Very sweet, but 'you' isn't going to sell soap. How about some words like…"

Like *that*. He squeezed himself, unable to fight the battle now.

He could have sworn she laughed. "Like…I don't know. I'm not very good at this. Luscious? Can you work with that?"

Her lips were luscious. If they would just close over him right…there… "Yeah, that's good, but…"

"I know, I know," she agreed. "Not good enough."

Not nearly, but he couldn't stop now. He pumped a little harder, fighting to hold back any sounds of his self-pleasuring, silently rocking his hips and wishing like hell he was rocking into her.

"Succulent?" she suggested.

Yes. Please suck it.

"Sweet?"

That would be so damn sweet.

"Oooh, how about tantalizing?" She dragged out the word, low and sexy and just enough to put him right over the edge. "Sultry? Sensual? Steamy and...Elliott? Elliott, don't you have any words for that fragrance?"

Yeah. Not anything that would go on a soap label. "Nothing terribly...soapy."

"Try harder."

"If you insist." Giving in completely, he leaned against the wall, biting his lip to keep from grunting, pumping furiously now. "It just isn't"—good enough—"real."

She laughed again. "Is anything that has your hands all over it?"

He looked up at the curtain, certain she was watching, but it held firm to the wall. Fire danced up his back and down his thighs, his whole body hot and hard and...finished. Biting his lip until he could taste blood, he shot an achy, unsatisfying, completely inauthentic load against the wall, momentarily satisfied, but hollow as hell.

Easy, yeah, but not good enough.

"Elliott? Are you okay?"

No, he wasn't okay. He was a shell of a man who wanted more than fake sex. Damn it! He wanted her, and he wanted it to be real. No matter how difficult it would be for a man who liked things easy.

"I said..." He cleared his throat and turned his hands under the stream, rinsing them. Finally, he inched the curtain back, but she wasn't there. "Frankie?"

"Right here."

He jerked around to see her at the other side of the shower, looking in. She raked him with a gaze that made him want to scream out in a wholly different kind of pain.

She gave him a hungry look, her gaze lingering on

his partial erection. "Maybe we should call that one Party of One."

He snapped the curtain closed and swore under his breath. "That name sucks." And so did a self-inflicted handjob when he wanted the real thing.

He heard her laughing as she left the bathroom.

Chapter Nine

"**B**ecker, is that woman biting you?" Nate slipped his sunglasses down his nose, just to get a better look at Elliott, but not far enough that anyone at the outdoor pavilion restaurant would recognize him.

Elliott brushed the mark on his arm, faded in the few days since Dominic had inflicted it. "Had a run-in with a buck."

On the other side of the table, Zeke leaned in. "A buck? Like a bronco?"

"A buck is what you call a male goat, Einstein."

Zeke and Nate shared a look, cracking up.

Elliott looked up at the deep blue sky and blew out an exasperated breath. He knew this lunch wouldn't be easy. They weren't going to like what he had to say, they weren't going to let him off the hook, and he hadn't really wanted to come to lunch at all. The days on the farm had slipped into a nice routine, next to Frankie from dawn to dusk, sneaking a few kisses whenever he could, laughing a lot, getting to know her. And, hell, he'd finally gotten promoted to the sofa at night.

Surely a move into the bedroom couldn't be far

away. It was inevitable, except…he couldn't do it until he got out from under the only dark cloud in his otherwise blissful week. And that's what he'd come to tell these guys, whether they liked it or not.

"What's so funny?" he demanded, taking a sip of a spicy Bloody Mary.

"It's just…" Zeke tried to keep a straight face but failed.

"It's you," Nate supplied. "Knowing about goats. If you don't think that's fucking hilarious, then you're dead inside."

But he wasn't dead inside. And that was the problem. For the first time in recent memory—and that went back years—Elliott felt completely alive. He wanted a woman in a way he'd never imagined possible. And he couldn't have her until his ill-conceived plan to screw her out of her land got killed.

"Goats happen to be very cool," he said. "And there's good money in goat's milk and the products. They're among the fastest-growing domestic animals in the world."

Zeke had to bite his lip, nodding, mirth dampening his eyes. "I'm sorry, Becker, but…*goats*?"

Ire and defensiveness zipped up his spine as he thought of all Frankie had been teaching him about goats this week. "They aren't just cute little weird animals, you know. People like to visit them. Kids love to pet them, and women buy the goat's milk products. And goat's milk—"

Zeke held up two hands in surrender. "Sorry, you're right." He couldn't wipe the smile off his face, though. "Really, that's good. You're right."

"Damn right I'm right," he said, reaching for his

drink but choosing cold water instead. His throat was parched with the pressing need to say what he had to say, hear them piss and moan about the change in plans, and get back to Frankie.

Nate seemed less amused by the goats, though it was hard to tell with his shades firmly in place in his never-ending effort to hide in a crowd. He rarely appeared in public without sunglasses, knowing every iPhone in the joint would be taking pictures and videos, and the line for autographs would form at the right. Maybe not in a classy place like Junonia, the outdoor restaurant near the pool at Casa Blanca, but for the most part, fame and the Ivory family fortune haunted Nate.

"You know what I think?" Nate said, leaning down just enough so his hazel eyes peered over the rims of his Ray-Bans. "I think something doesn't smell right, and it's not just the goats."

Nate might have been bad to the bone, spoiled rotten, and competitive to the point of death, but he was also surprisingly intuitive.

"What makes you say that?" Elliott asked, although he knew the answer, and he was grateful for the door his friend had opened for him.

"I think you're getting a little too cozy with the goat girl, and you're dreading the moment she finds out you screwed her in more ways than one."

"Just one," Elliott admitted. "I've only screwed her on paper." So far.

Nate and Zeke shared a look that said they didn't buy it. Well, too bad. It was the truth. He hadn't slept with her, but...he wasn't going to be able to hold off much longer. She'd made enough overtures and responded to enough kisses to know the feeling was more than mutual. The only thing stopping them now was the look on her face when she found out he'd slipped Ol' Comb-Over a deal on the side and stolen her property.

A white hot splash of self-loathing rolled through his gut.

But these weren't men who responded well to letting emotions get in the way of profit. Especially Nate. There had to be another way, an easy solution. Elliott always found the easy way...no matter how hard it was to spot.

He blew out a slow breath and turned to look at the beach and horizon on his right. "When you did the first site reviews, Zeke, did you talk to the owner of the land exactly to the east of the top end of her farm?"

Zeke shook his head. "It's scrub, utterly useless land."

"But who owns it?"

"I never bothered to look it up because the land didn't pass the most fundamental feasibility study. You're in the real estate business. You know useless land when you see it. You're the expert."

Someone had once told him a particular piece of land in Massachusetts was worthless because it was too hard to dig a foundation, and so far, that land had made him a very rich man. Feasibility studies could be proved wrong.

"I want to talk to the owner," he said.

"Don't bother," Zeke said. "The cost to clear that kind of land and make it usable for our needs would be astronomical."

Good. If a problem could be solved with money, it wasn't a problem. "But if we used that plot, she could keep her farm."

"No, she couldn't." Nate was pissed enough to take

his glasses off to make the point. "I was just in Miami with Flynn and saw a preliminary site drawing of the whole stadium complex. There is no physical way to follow any configuration that Flynn has had drawn up without putting parking somewhere on her land. And that's where it's going unless you're too whipped by a goat leash to put it there."

"Look, couldn't the parking somehow include her goat farm?" He'd been thinking about this, but hadn't yet put it into words. "It could attract tourists."

Nate hooted softly. "Yeah, 'cause people *always* want to stop at a goat farm when they go to a baseball game. Geez, Becker, I know we give you shit you about being a moron, but in this case, it might be true."

"But I—"

"He likes her," Zeke said, all the amusement gone from his eyes now, replaced by understanding and rationality. Thank God. "And he's trying to make her happy and give her what she wants."

Nate must have agreed, because he fell back in his chair and threw his hands up in resignation. "Well, there you go. Another one bites the dust."

"What dust?" Except Elliott knew exactly what dust he meant.

"Might as well start recruiting new team members for the Niners right now. Oh, hell, why don't we just change the name of the team to the Bucks? In honor of our goat-lover and former third baseman."

Elliott knew what Nate's comment meant. No one played on their softball team at home who wasn't rich and single. A walk down the aisle meant a walk off the team.

He shook his head. "I just met her," he said, and even

that level of denial felt wrong. "I mean, she's special, but…"

"Trust me," Zeke said. "When it happens, it happens fast."

"Are you and Mandy, uh…" Elliott tapped his left ring finger, unable to even say the word.

Zeke finally smiled. "Shopping for the rock this afternoon, buddy."

Nate let his forehead thud onto upturned palms. "What the hell is *wrong* with you two?"

"What's wrong with finding someone to spend your life with?" Zeke demanded.

"What's *right* with it?" Nate fired back, then he turned his disgust on Elliott. "She's a *goatherd*, for God's sake."

"Hey, Mandy was a maid," Zeke said, clearly coming over to Elliott's side in the conversation. "Look, why don't we look into other options before the deal that Becker set up goes through? Maybe we can do something with that other land."

He could tell Nate wanted to explode as he shook his head and no words came out. "Wait, wait," he sputtered. "Did you tell him about Will Palmer?"

"Who's that?" Elliott asked.

"He's a local," Zeke answered. "He's really involved with this resort, and his wife runs the spa. They're friends of Mandy's."

"What about him?" Elliott asked.

"Will Palmer." Nate dragged out the name like Elliott was an idiot for not recognizing it. "Former minor-league player, well connected, coaches, recruits, and absolutely loves the idea of baseball on Mimosa Key. He's already got some major names lined up to come to the announcement when we go public. He's going to bring in players from Miami and Tampa for an exhibition game right here at this resort, against the Niners, maybe in the next few weeks."

The announcement? An exhibition game with pros? In the *next few weeks*?

He could practically feel Frankie slipping through his fingertips.

"Whoa, whoa." He made a slow-down gesture with both hands. "Nate, we don't have that land deal yet. We can't *announce* anything."

Nate thunked his elbows on the table and stared at Elliott. "You want me in on the announcement?"

"Of course." They all knew that Nate added the glitz factor and that his family's name meant huge coverage for them.

"Well, my time is limited."

Elliott almost choked. His time? Time was all this trust-fund billionaire bad boy had. "Might have to reschedule a trip on your party barge to Greece this spring?" Elliott shot back.

Nate's jaw tensed as he gritted his teeth. "You're a riot, Elliott. We sent you down here to do a job. Do it or we can find someone else to take your place."

For a long, crazy minute, he thought about the offer. Really thought about Frankie and her farm and the goats and—

Zeke reached in to referee the argument. "We don't want to do this without Becker," he said to Nate. Then he turned to Elliott. "But I also don't want you to hurt someone you care about."

Elliott looked from one to the other. "She doesn't want to sell," he finally said. "The land has sentimental value to her."

"Sentimental value?" Nate's voice rose in shock. "Surely you offered enough money to crush any sentiment."

"It's *family* land, Nate. You understand family."

"I understand that I'd like to shoot mine." He curled his lip. "Did I say that?"

"Yeah." Elliott tilted his head toward the next table and lowered his voice. "And you better shut up or that'll be online in about three minutes."

"Listen to me." Nate pointed at Zeke, his voice low and soft. "You're thinking with your heart. And you"—he shifted the finger to Elliott—"are thinking with your dick. I guess that leaves me to use a brain."

"I am not," Elliott denied. If he had been thinking with his dick, he'd have had her in bed already instead of waiting to clean up this mess that he made first.

"Your tongue *is* hanging out to the floor," Zeke agreed.

Nate just shook his head, disgusted, as an older woman slowly approached their table, tentatively holding out a pen and paper. "Excuse me, but are you Nathaniel Ivory?"

He pushed his sunglasses back on, as if that could hide the truth.

"Could you..." She offered the pen to him.

Nate scratched his signature, but gruffly refused a picture. When she walked away, he threw back the rest of his champagne and pushed up. "Now it'll be all over Twitter that I'm an asshole who won't let my picture be taken. I'm out of here. If you need me, I'll be on my forty-million-dollar yacht. Or, as some call it"—he gave a lazy grin, softening his famous Ivory family jawline—"the party barge."

He walked away, sunglasses in place, body language set to *bother me and you die*.

"What's the bug up his ass?" Elliott asked Zeke when they were alone.

Zeke shrugged. "He's been acting strange. Lying even lower than usual. Maybe another Ivory family scandal on the horizon?"

"What day *isn't* there an Ivory family scandal on the horizon?"

Zeke looked around, frowning as he zeroed in on someone on the other side of the restaurant. "Hey, isn't that your goat girl?"

Elliott turned to see two women chatting under an awning, his gaze drawn to the familiar one. The beautiful one. The one he wanted more than his next freaking breath. How had that even happened to him? "She said she had a meeting here with—"

"Jocelyn Palmer," Zeke supplied.

"How'd you know that?"

"She's the one we were just talking about. Will Palmer's wife." Zeke frowned and gave Elliott's arm a warning tap. "Will knows about the baseball stadium, so it's a safe bet his wife does, too. And Will knew where we were going to put it, so…"

"So, shit." Elliott pushed up. "I should find an excuse to get those two apart."

Zeke pulled out his phone. "Good, you're leaving. I'll call Mandy." His voice was totally without sarcasm, just…happiness.

"It's good, isn't it?" Elliott asked.

Zeke beamed. "Like nothing I've ever known."

That hollow feeling that had gotten so familiar in the last few days deepened in his chest. "Do me a favor and look into that other land. I'll cover the clearing costs, no matter how astronomical they are. I'm getting out of the first deal I made."

"I will. I'll work on it this afternoon, but you have to do me a favor," Zeke replied.

"Whatever you need, buddy."

"Don't fight it."

Elliott knew exactly what the other man meant. "I'm...working on it."

"No, I mean it." Zeke stood up to level Elliott with a straight gaze. "You always go for the effortless way out of things. If it's real, it's worth doing the tough stuff, even if it hurts."

"Tough? I've been living in a trailer and cleaning up goat shit for her."

"It can get much tougher than that, my friend. Especially if you want it to be real."

Elliott turned again to look at her, just at the very moment she spotted him. Her face brightened, and her smile blinded and, damn it, his every nerve cell threatened to fry. Felt real enough.

"It is real," he said softly, unable to take his eyes off her.

"Not as long as you're lying to her, it's not."

His heart dropped a little. "Look, I'm going to tell her everything, but not until after I call that lawyer and kill the deal. It can't be pending, she'll never believe me. I'll track him down this afternoon and pull the offer that I put in."

"And then what?"

"Then I'll tell her and..." He finally turned to Zeke. "Who knows, Einstein? Maybe the Niners will be looking for two replacements."

Zeke gave him a nudge. "Get 'er done, cowboy."

Elliott snorted. "I'm no more of a cowboy than you are."

"But you are a straight shooter. If you want to talk to Burns first, do it, but make it right with her as soon as you can."

"I will." And he meant it.

Frankie's soaring heart rate had to be her excitement over how well the meeting had gone with the spa manager who'd walked her outside to say goodbye. It simply couldn't be the sight of Elliott Becker on the pavilion having lunch with his friend, his dark gaze locked on her like she was his one and only target.

Except he'd been looking at her a lot like that lately. And, every time, a thousand butterflies in her stomach made a mockery of her attempts to be cool. But cool had become warm, and warm was fast reaching the boiling point.

She wanted him. The kisses, the touches, the secret looks and sexy words and his poor, pathetic attempt to hide her effect on him in the shower…it had taken every ounce of self-control she'd ever had not to climb in there and finish the job for him and every time he'd taken a shower since then.

She'd been relieved when they'd gone off in different directions this morning, happy to have some time where her head didn't feel light and her limbs heavy with need.

"I know, it's amazing." The comment yanked Frankie

back to the moment, and she instantly returned her focus to Jocelyn Palmer, who was still holding and smelling some of the soap samples.

She closed her eyes and inhaled the mimosa and orange bar. "Mimosa Mornings," she said with a smile. "I just love how you've given these such incredible names and tied them all to the island. We could have so much fun with that!"

"I already have," Frankie said with a laugh.

"We are all about locally grown." Jocelyn's dark eyes gleamed with an inner peace and joy that Frankie already admired. "And romance," she said. "With so many destination weddings booked, I'd love to offer these perfectly named products in welcome gifts and baskets, if you're ready to ramp up production. Our brides might like them for wedding favors, too."

"I can be ready. I'm..." Frankie turned to follow Jocelyn's gaze, not the least bit surprised to see Elliott striding across the deck toward them, a black polo accentuating every muscle, even though it hung loose over casual cargo shorts.

He trotted down a few steps, extending a confident hand to Jocelyn. "You must be the spa manager Frankie was so excited to meet with today. I'm Elliott Becker."

The other woman's eyes widened a little, as if she knew the name. Well, he was technically a guest even if he hadn't spent one night in his villa.

"Hello, Mr. Becker, I'm Jocelyn Palmer."

"I see you're crazy about Frankie's amazing work."

"We were just talking about the great names they have," Frankie said, unable to resist leaning into him a little. "Here's the man to thank, Jocelyn.

He's a genius when it comes to that kind of thing."

"You have quite a way with words," Jocelyn agreed, but she kept looking at him, frowning slightly, and then she glanced at Frankie, obviously unsure of the connection.

"He's been visiting my farm for the last few days," Frankie said, hoping that would cover it.

"But aren't you part of the baseball thing? My husband is so thrilled about this—"

"Shhh." Still smiling, he put his finger over his lips. "We're really trying to keep it on the down low."

The baseball thing? Did she mean that the Niners were here? Frankie waited for an explanation, but Jocelyn was already nodding knowingly.

"I understand," she said. "But it won't stay quiet for long, not on this little island."

"We're trying, though. Are you two finished?" He gave an impatient tug to Frankie's hand, along with a look that said clearly how much he wanted to be alone with her.

"We were just playing with some ideas for more soap lines," Jocelyn said, missing the look completely. "Later this year, we have three wedding planners opening up a new bridal consulting firm in the resort, called Barefoot Brides, so we need to really amp up the romantic themes around here."

Elliott slid a comfortable arm around Frankie. "We can work on some romance," he teased.

Frankie laughed but couldn't bring herself to pull away. "I'm sure we can come up with all different themes and lines, Jocelyn."

"As you know, our resort motto is 'kick off your shoes and fall in love.'"

"We'll work on it." Elliott took a step away, effectively ending the meeting for her, his impatience palpable.

"Wait a second," Frankie said under her breath, giving him a warning look. He knew how important this meeting was to her, and it wasn't quite finished. "What's our next step, Jocelyn?"

"*Our* next step is the beach," Elliott replied. "Let's kick off our shoes and see what happens."

Jocelyn laughed. "Just call me as soon as you have the whole line ready to go," she said. "Oh, and Elliott, best of luck with the baseball project. It's going to mean great things for all of us and, honestly, I haven't seen my husband so excited since...well..." She looked down and tapped her loose-flowing top. "Since we found out some very good news."

"Oh!" Frankie exclaimed. "Congratulations! You certainly don't look pregnant."

"It's early yet, but we're very happy, thank you." She gave Frankie a spontaneous hug and whispered in her ear. "He looks like a keeper."

Frankie didn't reply but just said goodbye, her whole body warm from the sun and the encouragement. And the man who couldn't get much closer.

"So, she loved your soaps, huh?" he asked when Jocelyn went back inside.

She looked up at him, not that unhappy that he helped end the meeting. She wanted to be with him. "She loved your brilliant marketing, too. What's this about the baseball thing?"

That glorious smile faltered for a second. "Hey, can we walk the beach or are you afraid the slogan's really a prediction?"

"I'm not afraid of anything except an expertly changed subject to avoid answering."

He laughed, his easy, breezy, I-can-make-anyone-do-what-I-want laugh that Frankie had already learned to discern from his real laugh. The difference, she'd figured out after many hours with him, was in his eyes. Right now, they might be on her, but something was flat in his gaze.

"No expert anything," he denied. "You know some of my softball teammates are here. And you know one of them is Nate Ivory."

"Yes?"

"Well, he hates publicity, as you can imagine."

"Gets enough of it, though."

He nudged her out from under the awning and gestured toward the beach. "Kick off your shoes, Frankie."

And fall in love.

She toed off her sandals, and he did the same to his Docksiders and took her hand as they stepped onto the warm, fine sand.

"So why would Jocelyn's husband be so excited about you guys being here?"

"He's a former pro ball player and..." Elliott looked out at the horizon, his voice fading as he seemed to get lost in thought.

"And?" she prompted.

He turned and looked down at her, his expression so serious she drew back. "And..." He swallowed, searching her face, his seriousness growing downright dark.

"What is it, Elliott?"

"And we..." He shook his head. "It's not important.

It's just some dumb baseball stuff." Before she could respond, he pulled her into his chest, wrapping his arms around her and dropping a kiss on her hair. "Tell me about your meeting with Jocelyn. Tell me about your plans for the farm. That's what's important."

Closing her eyes, she let the moment wash over her. The sand in her toes, the man in her arms, the lightness in her heart.

"What's important, huh? You're awfully philosophical. Did you drink at lunch?"

He laughed. "Busted. One Bloody Mary. You want one?"

She let out a soft moan, her head dropping back at how awesome that sounded. "Yes. Let's go." She turned back to the patio restaurant, where her gaze landed on his friends, sitting at a side table, deep in conversation.

"I knew he'd come back," Elliott muttered, steering her in the opposite direction.

"Don't you want to join them? They're looking right at us."

"Let them. Come on, I have a better idea." He rounded the deck, scooped up their shoes and led her to the back of the resort to the shaded, paved road that ran from the hotel to each of the private villas.

At the main entrance, he snagged a golf cart, offered a hand to help her up, and drove away toward his villa, uncharacteristically silent.

He definitely didn't want her talking to his friends.

"Are you really worried that I might be attracted to Nathaniel Ivory?" she asked, not sure what to make of that character trait if it were true.

"No," he said simply, his jaw set in a way she wasn't sure she'd seen before.

Without asking what was wrong, she hung on as the cart rumbled past picturesque villas, each tucked into their own tropical gardens. Some had front verandas that faced the bay with completely private pools in the back. Others were situated so that their elevated pools offered bay views. All of them were gorgeous, including the last one, Rockrose.

He turned to her, not climbing out of the golf cart. "Come inside with me so we can talk."

Talk? They'd been talking for days. "Okay," she said, leaning closer. "If you want to talk." She kissed him lightly. "But I'm kinda talked out today."

He fought a smile, a battle waging in his eyes, but still she couldn't figure out why he seemed so conflicted. She was practically inviting herself into his bed.

"We can talk, too," he said.

She smiled and lifted a shoulder. "Whatever you want." She started to slide her leg out of the cart, but he gripped her arm, holding her there.

"Francesca."

Her heart slipped around, helpless, as it always did, when he used her full name.

"I really like you," he said.

"I really like you, too."

"No, I mean..." He exhaled, frustration oozing off him. "I want to talk and tell you..."

"Hey." She wrapped her arms around his neck and pulled him close, putting her lips right over his ear. "I got a bag full of sweet-smelling cotton balls that I need you to name."

He grinned. "If that's not the sexiest offer I've ever had, then I don't know what is."

"This." She covered his mouth with a kiss, as hard

and hot and sincere as she could make it, and he melted almost immediately. At least, his strange arguments melted. Nothing else melted.

Only her heart when he scooped her up and carried her inside, refusing to put her down or end the kiss until she was lying on his bed, breathless and ready for him.

Chapter Ten

What the hell was wrong with him? Elliott's body was ready—so, so damn hard and ready—but something in his chest, probably in the vicinity of his heart or, *worse*, his soul, wouldn't make a move. Instead, Elliott slowly sat on the giant king-size bed.

"So, where are these fragrances?" he asked.

From under her thick lashes, she eyed him suspiciously. "In my bag, which I dropped in the entryway when you Rhett Butlered me into bed and then…changed your mind."

"I didn't…" Shit. "I want to help you with your fragrances."

With a soft sigh, she rolled off the bed and disappeared out the bedroom door. For a moment, he froze, wondering if she'd just given up on him completely. And part of him was hoping she had. He could call Burns, kill the deal, and then, and only then, could he get in this bed with Francesca and probably stay in it for a week.

Ah, hell, he hated when shit that should have been easy got all complicated and difficult.

"Damn it," he muttered, falling back on the bed and throwing an arm over his face. Who *was* he?

"Smell." Frankie's hand closed over his arm, keeping it firmly over his eyes as a heady and rich aroma hit his senses. She straddled him on the bed without taking the cotton ball from under his nose. "How's that?"

"Nice." He used his one free hand to push her a little lower and get right over his... "Really damn nice."

"What's it smell like to you?"

"My sense of smell just gave in to my sense of"—he rocked his hips against her bottom—"woman."

Just a little, a traitorous voice whispered in his head. Just a few kisses and touches and maybe he could tell her without...

No. He had to do this right.

"I'm serious, Elliott."

Sadly, so was he. He would not...how had Nate put it? Screw her in more ways than one. He wasn't going to be that guy.

But then she rolled a little harder over his erection. "What's this smell like?"

Heaven. Trouble. Fun. *Frankie.*

He caressed her backside and hip, letting his fingers wander to the front of her skirt, skimming skin under her thin cotton top. "It smells like...coconut."

"Yeah, but what does it make you think of?" Her stomach was taut and silky and tensed up at his light touch. "Remember the assignment. Romance."

Romance. And until he was honest and real, this wasn't romance. This was...the tip of his finger glided over the bottom of a lacy bra. This was sex.

Which used to be just fine, thank you very much.

"I don't know," he said gruffly, yanking his hand away.

She tsked. "Losing your touch, Becker?"

He wanted to smile, but nothing was funny, not even her stupid pun. "What is this stuff?" he asked, trying to play along and remember the labels he'd read on the vials. "Lemon verbs or something?"

She laughed, tightening her legs, her bare calves against his thighs, and little else except that slip of a frilly skirt she wore. What else did she not have on under that skirt?

His dick grew harder, right into her bottom, earning a sweet little moan from her when she felt it.

"It's clearly making you think of something romantic."

"It makes me think of..." Sex. Sweet, fast, easy, hard, *now*. "Lavender?" he guessed.

"Becker," she sighed in frustration and lifted her hand so he could look up at her. She rested her hands on either side of his head, her hair dangling down to his cheeks, her top draped enough that he could easily slide his hand right...up...there.

"I need you to work your magic," she said.

Magic. She was magic. He put both hands on her hips and rolled her over his erection. And that was magic. Hot, needy, achy magic.

"Come and kiss me, Francesca."

On a sigh that sounded like pure relief, she lowered herself and pressed against him, kissing soft and sweet before adding heat and passion.

One hand found its way under her top, caressing skin as he reached around to unhook her bra and fill his hand with her bare breast. The other was already bunching up the skirt, desperate for skin and a long-awaited caress of her backside.

She was just as hungry and desperate, whimpering with each kiss, nibbling his jaw, threading her fingers through his hair, his name on her lips between strangled breaths.

"We never got a name for midnight, remember?" she said in between kisses, giving him the cotton.

He laid her on her back, bracing himself on one elbow next to her, lifting her hair to find that delicate spot right under her ear. "Let me smell it on you. That inspires me." He dabbed the fragrance gently, leaning in to kiss her eyes and cheeks and mouth.

And then back to look at how incredibly beautiful she was.

She looked at him. "How does it smell?"

"I need to find another place." He reached down to her skirt, pulling it higher to reveal her long thigh and bare hip. As he stared at her gorgeous body, his own nearly exploded. She wore nothing but a tiny strip of white satin, a thong he could take off with his teeth. "A place right…here," he said gruffly, drinking in the sight of her, trailing the cotton to a sweet spot on her inner thigh.

He lowered his head, loving that she guided him and pulled his hair just enough to show how much she wanted this, letting him kiss her hip and that wisp of material.

"Let me test it here."

"O…kay." She could barely talk, so he stole a peek at her face, eyes closed, mouth slack, her expression rapture and anticipation.

He could do this, right? This wasn't *everything*. They would do everything after he…after this.

He inched the tiny triangle of white to the side,

revealing her sex-slick womanhood. He lowered his head, then dabbed her with the oil-scented cotton ball.

She sucked in a breath and let go of his hair, clutching the comforter instead.

Closer, he inhaled a mix of woman and lavender, of sex and spice. Very carefully, he kissed her and then slid his tongue around and around.

"Becker." She rocked up to meet his mouth. "Oh, God, don't stop."

Dividing his gaze between her heavy-lidded eyes and the visual of beautiful woman, he licked warm skin, curling his tongue then stroking her with feathery brushes of cotton, teasing her closer to abandon.

She gripped his shoulder, called out his name, and bucked against his mouth with the first full shudder of release. He pulled it from her, sucking and licking and holding her hips until she exploded with an orgasm.

She whispered his name, the sound of satisfaction and delight while her whole body quivered. She tried to pull him up, but barely had the strength, so he kissed his way back to her mouth.

"Becker, what do you call *that* fragrance?"

He laughed. "Well, I call it..." He couldn't even think of a word good enough to giving Frankie that kind of pleasure. "Where I belong."

She finally opened her eyes enough to let him see her surprise. "Not a very...soapy name from my marketing guru."

"What would you call it?"

"Amazing. Perfection. A prelude to...something."

They both knew exactly what something that was a prelude to.

"How about a prelude to a promise?" he suggested. "Too corny?"

"Well, it's for weddings planners. They love corny."

They both laughed, and she reached her hand to stroke his cheek. "I like you, Becker. So much it scares the hell out of me."

"What are you scared of, Francesca?"

She sighed and closed her eyes. "Everyone I love leaves me."

The admission was so simple and true, it hit like a punch between the eyes. He didn't even know how to respond, so he just lay down next to her, ignoring his body's needs to take this moment to connect.

"What are *you* scared of, Elliott?"

He thought for a long time, holding her hand, letting their heart rates settle back to normal.

"You *are* going to tell me the truth and be real, aren't you?" she asked.

"Yes." But not yet. He couldn't tell her yet. He'd have to tell her another kind of truth. A different revelation. "I'm scared that no matter what I do or where I go or how much I spend or make or accumulate, I will never be…" *Where I belong.* "Home."

She sat up slowly, leaning on her elbow to look at him. "Tell me why."

And for the first time ever, he wanted to tell someone everything. All his pain, all his missing parts, all the reasons why he had a hard time being real.

Because with this woman, being real was easy. Too easy. He'd never even thought there was such a thing.

Yes, Frankie wanted to have sex with Elliott Becker. More sex. Real sex. But something was stopping him, and Frankie suspected he just wanted one last wall to come down between them. He wanted to tell her something. That had been clear for a while now. And she wanted to tell him something, too.

So sex could wait. She had a feeling there'd be plenty, and often. This sharing was far more important.

They were both still fully clothed, but he nestled her into him, sliding a powerful leg over hers. He gently eased her head into the space right over his heart, his chin against her hair.

For a long time, neither spoke. Their breaths slipped into an easy unison, the afternoon sunlight slipping through plantation shutters to stream warmth on them. Frankie felt everything tense and scary and unhappy lift from her heart for the first time in a long time.

"Home," he finally said. He nodded, as though that sounded right to him. "I'd like a home."

She pushed up on her elbows again, certain she'd misunderstood the whispered words. "Didn't you say you have a few already?"

"I've got an apartment in New York and I keep a place in Paris, just because, I don't know. It's pretty there. My parents retired to San Diego, so I have a place there, and I like to ski so I bought a house in Aspen. And, of course, my gold mine in Massachusetts, but I don't live there. My place in Boston is in Beacon Hill."

She laughed softly. "Okay. What's wrong with this picture? You just told me of, what, five, maybe six different places you own and none of them are home? You live there, right? And something tells me that 'apartment' in New York isn't a walk-up."

"It's nine thousand square feet, three stories, with five different balconies and a three-sixty-degree view of New York City."

"Holy crap," she muttered.

"And by the way," he said softly, not breaking the slow stroke of her hair. "I looked up the quote. Money isn't the root of all evil. It's the *love* of money that's the root of all evil."

"Who said that? Shakespeare?"

"God. It's in the Bible."

"Really." She hadn't known that. "Still doesn't change my feeling about it or the fact that you own all that real estate and still don't have a place to call home."

"Because calling a house a home doesn't make it one," he said. "Now don't get me wrong, I love my places. But you'll never hear me call them home. The apartment in New York is jaw-dropping, I know. I have great parties there, and I actually live in about one-fifth of it, which includes the kitchen, bedroom, and media center. But..." He shook his head. "Nope, not my idea of a home."

"What is?"

"I don't know." He was quiet for a few seconds, thinking. "I started to think this week that..." His voice trailed off, and she didn't dare look up to see his face to figure out what he was thinking. Because if he was thinking...

No. Crazy fantasies. *Stop it, Francesca.*

"...that it must be nice to have something that's been in your family and has history like that."

Not exactly where she'd thought he might be going, that he might admit *her* home felt like it could possibly be *his* home.

128

"I've never lived anywhere for more than eighteen months," he said. "And now, I don't live in one place for more than a month or two before I jet off to the next apartment or house. I never had 'a room of my own,' a structure full of memories, or, you know, that place where you fall, where you can be..." His voice faded, and then he laughed softly. "A place where I can be myself."

She smiled at him, getting it completely. "So that's why you're a chameleon. You need a home base." Deep in her chest, so deep it was like a little black hole she'd never expected to find, a low, slow burn heated up, even though it terrified her. What if...could she be...was there a chance to make a home with a man like this?

"So why not build a house in the burbs and live there?" she asked quickly, trying to plug up that sensation.

"I don't know if I want that, either."

She slid her arm all the way around him, holding on to his substantial body, warm and close and so, so comfortable. "I think, ladies and gentlemen, that we have found ourselves a man who can have everything but doesn't know what he wants."

"You know..." He looked at her, his whole expression soft. "You're so damn right. I want..." His voice faded and, suddenly, a guard went up. Imperceptible, but she knew it.

"You want what?"

He didn't answer, still slicing her with his dark gaze, something—a lot—going on in his head.

"You're lucky, you know that?" he asked.

"Because I don't have that pesky pied-à-terre in Paris or the nine-thousand-square-foot place to keep clean?"

"Because you found a place where you...belong. I want that. I don't care if it's fancy or impressive or what people think I *should* be living in. I just want it to be a place where..." He shook his head, laughing. "This is cheeseball, but I want it to be a place where my heart is."

Her own heart took a dip and a dive. "That's where the person you love is," she whispered.

"Like your Nonno was."

Not exactly what she was thinking, but he'd opened a door she needed to step through. "Speaking of Nonno..."

She felt his gaze on her as she stared ahead, not willing to look in his eyes.

"What?"

"That promise I made?"

He shifted a little closer. "Yeah?"

She turned flat on her back and stared up at the ceiling, aware that her heart thumped with the need to be honest. She'd asked for him to be real and now she had to be, too.

"Frankie?"

"That night that I talked to my grandfather..." Biting her lip, she let the words fade with her next breath.

"Yeah?" He took her hand and gently, softly rubbed her knuckles with his much-larger fingers. She lifted their joined hands to look at his.

"Have I told you how attractive I find your hands?" she asked.

He squeezed her fingers. "Illegal change of subject."

She nodded, building up more courage. She owed him this truth. "It was about four in the morning, and I was with him in the ICU. The halls were so quiet and still. I wouldn't leave his side even though he was deep

130

in a coma. There were no nurses in the room, just Nonno and me."

She closed her eyes, her whole focus on the warm place where their hands touched, transported back to that dark hospital room, the only sounds the steady beep of the machines monitoring Nonno's heart. She'd held his hand, too, just like this. But instead of the strong, young, powerful hand of Elliott Becker, she'd grasped the frail, wrinkled, sunspotted fingers of her Nonno. "I remember bending over to put my head against his chest, just to close my eyes for a moment and hear his heart. I knew his time was…close."

For a moment, neither spoke as she remembered the slightly antiseptic smell of Nonno's hospital gown and the thin bones of his old chest against her cheek. "And then he said, 'Don't ever let our land go, *piccolina*.'"

"When he woke up?"

And there was the rub. She looked up at Elliott. "I…think so. Maybe. I'm not sure." She took a slow, long breath. "He never opened his eyes, but his voice was clear and so was our conversation. But…he died." She swallowed hard. "I think he died before we had that conversation."

Elliott just looked at her, clearly not quite getting where she was going.

"I fell asleep after we talked…" At least, she thought she had. "And I woke up when the nurses came running in, and they said…he was gone. They told me he'd never come out of the coma because they would have known it. They told me…I imagined the whole conversation, but I talked to him, I know I did. I heard him and he heard me and we…talked."

Hadn't they? Sometimes it was hard to be absolutely certain.

And if it had never happened, how much weight could she put on that promise?

"Then the nurses were wrong," he said, at least *acting* like he believed her.

She sighed. Deep in her heart, she knew that they couldn't have been, but... "Sometimes, I think that he was already...gone." She shook her head, the memory of that conversation so vivid it *couldn't* have been a dream.

"So..." He got up on his elbow, looking down at her. "What you're saying is you aren't sure if you really made that promise or not?"

She didn't answer for a long, long time, then finally, she nodded. "It might have been, you know, my imagination."

He stroked her cheek, silent, thinking. "No, it wasn't. And you're lucky, then." He leaned closer and kissed her. "You've talked to angels."

Her heart folded in half and then burst in her chest. "Yes," she said, fighting tears. "I have."

"I'm lucky, too."

"So you've said a million times."

He smiled at her. "You talk to them. I get to fall in..."

She waited. What would he say? In love? In bed? In—

On the floor, her cell phone rang inside the bag she'd brought in, shredding the moment. She huffed out a breath of frustration, but he gave her a nudge.

"You can get that."

"No, I—"

"Really, you can get it." He leaned over the bed and snagged her bag, flipping it up on the bed. "It's the middle of the day and...it could be Jocelyn."

Did he want this intimate conversation to come to a crashing halt? It sure seemed so.

"Plus, I have something important I have to do today." He pulled her phone out of the side pocket and handed it to her, pushing himself off the bed.

Had they gone too far? Revealed too much? Bewildered, she took the phone and barely glanced at the screen, half-registering that it was Liza Lemanski from the County Clerk's office.

Before she could sit up to answer, Elliott was halfway across the room, and then he disappeared into the bathroom, closing the door. Frowning and ignoring the punch of disappointment in her chest, she tapped the screen and answered the phone.

"Hi, Liza."

"If you tell anyone I made this call, I will deny it until they tie me up and hang me in red tape."

Any other time, she'd have laughed. But... Frankie stared at the closed door and reached behind herself to hook her bra, a flush of embarrassment rising even though Liza couldn't possibly know where she was. "Your secret's safe. What's up?"

"I found the will. And the property deed."

"That's go—"

"And the multimillion-dollar offer from a third party that is set to close in forty-eight hours."

"*What*?"

"I'm not kidding, Frankie, someone has made a cash offer, and it is going through fast, fast, fast. That Burns guy has a one hundred percent legitimate will that your grandfather must have signed in a moment of weakness. He works for some seedy company that preys on old people who don't have official wills."

"Is that legal?"

"It isn't illegal if no one contests the will or they unload the property before a family member gets involved. And that's what Burns is doing. He's sold it to the highest bidder for so much more than market value, it should be a crime."

"How much?"

"I don't even want to tell you because I can't stand to hear a grown woman cry."

Oh, God. No. "How much?"

"More than you can beat, unless you have a few million or ten stashed away. Who even has that kind of money?"

She stared at the door. Elliott did. A man who could be...unreal.

"Who's the buyer?" she asked, the metallic taste of dread and shame filling her mouth.

"I can't—"

"Liza, please. You have to tell me. I have a feeling I just...I almost had sex with him." And, worse, dreamed of a future.

"Oh, God, I hate men. Have I told you how much I hate men? Hate."

"Liza?"

"The name is Becker. Elliott A. Becker. I'm guessing the A is for Asshole."

Frankie closed her eyes as the blow hit her heart. "You'd be guessing right," she muttered, already scooping up her bag and turning to the door. "Let me ask you something, Liza." She kept her voice low as she tiptoed down the hall to the living room.

"Sure. I've broken every rule in the County Clerk's bylaws and employee handbook by calling you. What's one more?"

Very quietly, without making a sound, she turned the front doorknob. "Can you give me a phone number for that Burns guy?"

"I…can't."

"He gave me his card, but I…" Left it in a place for Elliott Becker to find. Damn him! "Liza, please."

Outside, she slid into the golf-cart seat and reached for the start button. "I have to do this," she whispered, hating the catch in her throat.

"Can you write it down?"

"I won't forget it. I won't forget anything." Like just how close she'd come to being screwed in every way possible.

The electric cart barely made a sound as she rolled toward the paved road, memorizing the number Liza gave her before they hung up. But just as she passed the next villa, she heard her name, loud and clear.

"Frankie! Damn it, Frankie, where are you going?"

Feet slammed on the pavement behind her, but she gunned the cart and swerved around some shocked resort guests.

"Francesca Cardinale, stop that cart and listen to me!"

Did he have no idea who he was dealing with? Was he so shortsighted that he didn't think she could beat him at his own game of pretend?

"Frankie, please! I'm sorry! I want you! I belong with you!"

You belong in hell, Becker.

She shoved her hand in the air, thrust her middle finger to the sky, and kept driving.

Chapter Eleven

Voice mail. Voice mail. Voice fucking mail. Then nothing. The damn thing didn't even ring anymore.

It was like Michael S. Burns, attorney-at-law, no longer existed. Elliott flung the business card on the bed, tossed the phone on top of it, and let himself follow both, stuffing his face into the blankets that an hour later still smelled like…

Where I belong.

Except he didn't belong anywhere, especially not in the arms of a genuine, amazing, one-of-a-kind angel who deserved so much more than a fake. Because that's all Elliott Becker was. A phony, manipulative bastard who thought he could hedge his bets and play both ends against the middle and every other gambling cliché that always worked for him because it was easy and he was lucky.

Not anymore.

Now he was the empty shell of a fool who'd made a mistake and couldn't cover it up.

He flipped over, staring at the ceiling. Who'd called her? Burns? Why would he do that? Someone had found out. Maybe Jocelyn Palmer had alerted her. Hell, maybe Nate had sabotaged this.

At the thought, he shot up, furious and ready to kill his friend.

That would be just like that spoiled prick who got everything he wanted. Probably thought if he wrecked the romance, then Elliott would go ahead with the—

Three hard raps at the front door of the villa pushed him to his feet. If that was Nate, he might punch the bastard. If it was Zeke, maybe he could help. Elliott had to do something. He had to track the guy down and withdraw the offer and then go grovel in the hay and beg for—

"Mr. Becker! It's Michael Burns!"

Burns. Elliott whipped open the door and stared at the weasel with a comb-over, relief nearly buckling his knees. Thank God, his luck still held in some regards.

"Get in here." Elliott grabbed the guy's arm and practically yanked him. "I've been calling you nonstop for an hour!"

"Sorry. I was in a bank vault, and that cuts off the signal to my phone."

"I need to—"

"Here's your check, Mr. Becker."

Elliott stared at it, then closed his eyes. This transcended lucky. This was downright miraculous. "So you got my message that I wanted to end the deal before you finalized any paperwork?"

"Oh, I finalized plenty of paperwork, sir. The deal went through an hour ago."

Shit! "Then why are you giving me this check back?"

"Not your deal. I sold the land to the highest bidder, and I must say, that bidder doubled your offer with hard, cold cash. I honestly didn't think it was worthwhile to try to get you to counter."

Her land was gone? "No, you didn't sell it! You can't sell it!" He practically dove on the guy. "Whatever the amount, whatever it is, I'll beat it." He'd buy it back and give it to her. She couldn't lose La Dolce Vita. It was where she belonged. And where he—

"My deal's done. You can work with the new buyer, but I doubt she'll budge an inch. That woman laid down more money than I ever dreamed I could get and, between you and me, way more than it's worth. I have other—"

"Who bought it?" Except, he kind of knew, didn't he? In fact, who else would buy it?

"That squatter with the goats." Burns shook his head. "You just never know who has money, do you? I peeked over the bank manager's shoulder and got a whiff of her net worth." He leaned forward, eyes wide. "I could have sworn there were nine goose eggs in that number. Can you imagine?"

Yes, he could imagine. He could very well imagine that a girl who'd come from extreme wealth and never touched the money, investing it wisely for over a decade, maybe hitting some gold of her own, would have "some money" stashed away, as she'd said. Rare, unlikely, but who knew better than him how the right investment could pay off?

"Listen, pal, I have more land all over Florida that I—"

Elliott yanked himself back to the weasel in front of him. "Is it all land you scammed out of old people with no wills?"

"Not all of it and…and I don't do the visits or

138

anything, I just handle the legal stuff. There are guys tougher than me that visit these old folks and try to scam them."

Elliott leaned into his face, taking the guy's collar in his hands. "Don't you have a grandparent, pal? What the hell's wrong with you?"

He tried to shake Elliott off, his face paling. "I need a job, man. I have bills and…problems."

"You want money? I'll pay you to get me the name of your dirtbag clients and a list of the people they're scamming. Then I'll pay you to be the lawyer for those poor old people and you won't have any problems."

His eyes widened. "Really?"

Elliott exhaled, shaking his head. "Problems that can be solved with money aren't problems, pal."

But his couldn't be solved with any amount of money. He took a slow step backward, trying to process all of this. Frankie had her land, so that was good. And he had…nothing.

Without her, he was right back to where he really belonged…nowhere.

"I'm serious," he finally said to Burns. "You have my number. Call my office." When the man left, Elliott stood in the middle of the living room, staring at the check. Millions of dollars that didn't matter to anyone without…a home, a partner, love.

How could he ever make her see that he understood that now?

He didn't know how, but he knew one thing. It wasn't going to be easy.

After Frankie returned home from the bank, she forgot about Elliott Becker. It took absolutely no willpower, because something else had completely captured her attention. Isabella was in labor.

Fortunately, she'd been feeling the doe's right side every day and had noticed some tension and change in the shape. Remembering how Nonno had handled the kid births when she was young, Frankie had prepared a clean stall with a bed of short-cut hay so it was extra soft, and had all the does milked and dogs fed, making them stay outside while she watched Isabella.

She had gloves and K-Y Jelly in case of breech, and a spool of thread, as well as lots and lots of towels. Since a goat could give birth to a kid on a mountainside with no boiling water, sterilized tools, or human in sight, there was little to do but make sure all went well and that her kids—she had no idea how many were in there—were all born alive.

Sometimes, intervention was necessary, but Frankie was certain she could handle it. And grateful for something other than Elliott Becker to think about. She cooed at the bleating goat, looking for the signs that she'd be delivering soon. Ears out, flank distended, some seriously gross stuff coming out of her.

"I think we're ready, Izzie," she whispered. "How many are in there, girl? We need a lot for our amazing farm, don't we?"

The farm she'd have without...him.

Grunting at herself, she focused on the doe. Her best guess was that Isabella had been in labor all day, so it wouldn't be too long now. Poor thing. She'd been here alone, while Frankie...was being had.

She stomped on the ugly thought and refused to let

herself wallow in pity or sadness. It was over. She was done with Elliott Becker, and if and when he showed up to toss around his empty lies and phony words, she would tell him that. Now, she had to watch Isabella, who was pacing the stall, stomping, whining, and occasionally looking up for relief that Frankie couldn't offer.

Leaning against the wall, she tried to soothe Isabella by petting her, but the goat bleated and dug at the hay, over and over again, until her hind legs folded under her.

"You ready to go, girl?"

Isabella cried out and rolled onto her side, laying out her leg to make room. Suddenly, she jerked sideways and yelped.

Intervention time.

Frankie yanked on gloves and squeezed the jelly all over her hands, the whole time whispering and calming a very unhappy and uncomfortable doe. Outside, the dogs kicked up their barks, as if they knew something was wrong, but she blocked it all out as she reached for the doe's leg, sucking in a breath when a stream of blood trickled out. "Oh my God."

Should she call the vet and leave her alone? Or go in there and—

"Frankie!"

She jerked up at the sound of her name.

"Where are you?"

Becker. Thank God. Right now, she'd take help from Satan himself. "In the back. The birthing stall. Isabella's in trouble!"

She heard his boots hit the shelter floor, hating herself for how much she'd gotten used to that sound, and learned to love it.

141

"What's wrong?" He was next to her in an instant, the strength and security of him almost bowling her over as he reached out instinctively for the doe.

"No, wash your hands. Get gloves. No, no. Call the vet."

And then he was gone, taking her orders as Isabella screamed bloody murder.

"Where's your cell?" Becker asked from behind her. "Is the vet's number on it?"

"Yes, yes. My pocket." She reached her back pocket, finally looking at him for the first time. Holy mother, he looked like hell.

"Here, give me the phone," he said. "What's the name?"

Isabella bayed again. "Wait, wait. I need to find out if she's breech. Can you hold her legs open?"

He was on his knees, gloved hands reaching out with a surprising amount of tenderness, his face next to Frankie's. "Like that?" he asked.

Why did her damn heart slip around like that? She hated him. He'd screwed her—or tried to. "Yes. Let me reach in there." She looked up at him, expecting a curled lip of disgust, but he looked at Isabella with sympathy, touching her gently.

After a moment, she found the back end of the kid. "She's breech. I have to turn the kid."

"You want me to call the vet?"

She shook her head. "We can do this." She'd meant *I* can do this, but there he was, next to her, a partner, a friend, a lover... "An asshole who tried to steal my land."

"Now, Frankie?"

She almost laughed, except Isabella was howling

with pain. "Sorry. Later." She pushed and prodded, sweat trickling over her face as she made careful, slow moves that wouldn't tear the placenta.

The whole time, Elliott held Isabella's legs. He talked to her and stroked her sweetly and, damn, if he didn't calm the doe down between contractions and give Frankie a chance to turn the kid.

Suddenly, a yellow bubble appeared.

"What's that?" he asked in horror.

Now she did laugh. "That's the placenta. And inside there, look…" A tiny brown foot came out first, then the face of a very pretty goat. "There's our first kid."

Both of them were silent as Isabella pushed quietly, the wee baby sliding out with its gooey overcoat.

"And maybe not our last."

The way he said it…whoa. She didn't dare look at him, didn't dare give away how that got to her. "Most times there are two," she said. "But there could be three or four or five. You ready, cowboy?"

The rest of a little brown goat plopped onto the hay, making both of them suck in a simultaneous breath.

"Would you look at that?" Elliott whispered, awe and a crack in his voice. "Even a goat birth is a miracle."

She finally found the strength to look at him again, inches away, his expression all dark and tortured and pained. He returned the gaze, the two of them inches away but worlds apart.

"Frankie," he whispered. "Is there any possible way you'll accept a simple apology?"

She managed a smile. "No." Then she turned back to Isabella. "But it looks like we've got another. And this one's coming out just as it should."

Isabella seemed to calm after she had a chance to

greet her new baby girl with mama licks, and then she relaxed for the next delivery.

Frankie gathered her towels and gently cleaned the kid and got her ready for the tiny warm bed she'd prepared. For now, though, she let the baby stay near her mama.

Elliott cleared his throat against the silence. "I guess you'll never believe me if I tell you I was going to withdraw my offer."

She patted the tiny kid's head. "You'd guess right, then."

He sighed. "Well, I was."

Without answering, she laid a hand on Isabella's leg, feeling it tense for the second delivery. She shouldn't ask questions. She shouldn't give an inch, because this was Elliott Becker, and he'd charm and flirt and tease and lie his way to forgiveness that she had no intention of giving.

"So why didn't you tell me?" she asked, apparently unable to hear the rational voice in her head.

"I was going to, once I'd…undone my mistake." He leaned closer, but she refused to look. "That's why I didn't…why we didn't…"

"We did enough," she finished for him. Enough for her to feel like they'd had sex and she'd offered him her body…and all the time, he'd known he was trying to steal her land. "Enough for me to be hurt."

"I'm sor—"

She held up her hand and looked at him. "No amount of groveling in the world will allow me to trust you again."

He closed his eyes as if the words had been a direct hit.

"I know this isn't going to change things, Frankie, but—"

"Then don't say it. Just…" She shook her head. "You really don't need to be here."

"I need to explain a few things to you."

She exhaled slowly, peering down to see the next kid just starting to make an appearance.

"My friends, Nate and Zeke, we're joining forces to build a baseball stadium and start a minor-league team here."

Very slowly, she turned her head, the words flowing over her like a bucket of ice. "You wanted to build a baseball stadium on Nonno's Dolce Vita?" Surely he heard the dismay in her voice.

"Actually, the stadium's going to be over there, farther west. This land was for the"—he swallowed hard—"parking lot and access road."

She actually laughed because, how the hell else should she react to that? "Why not the men's room, while you're so busy demeaning my precious legacy of land?"

"But we could change that," he said quickly. "I've been thinking about a way to change that."

"By finding some other piece of land on some other island that's owned by some other unsuspecting, lonely, stupid, easily manipulated female?"

He just stared at her. "You're lonely, Frankie?"

Damn it. "No, I'm not," she ground out. "And notice how you didn't correct 'stupid'?"

"Because I know you're not stupid, but if you are lonely…" He reached for her, and she jerked away as if his hand were made of fire. His beautiful, large, sexy hand that she wanted…

Oh, Lord, have the kid already, Isabella!

"What if we worked the farm into the stadium?"

She blinked at the tiny baby in front of her, barely able to process the question. "Like a seventh-inning stretch and goat parade? What the hell, Becker?"

"I'm serious." He got a little closer, his dark eyes flashing like they did when he had some brilliant, grandiose, ridiculous idea that always ended up being...perfect. "We could have your whole idea for a stone house and a little store, maybe a petting zoo for the kids."

She frowned at him. "You're nuts, you know that?"

"Not if the team were called the Barefoot Bay Bucks. Then the goats would be mascots. It's amazing, don't you think?"

"Certifiable." She shook her head and pointed to Isabella. "Shhh. Here comes another one."

Just as slowly, but with much less drama, a little brown and white face emerged, protected by a shiny bubble. Isabella bleated with relief as the shoulders came through, then the backside. The kid plopped onto the hay with a soft thud.

"Would you look at that?" Elliott whispered. "We had a boy."

She gave a sad smile. "I might be able to keep one."

"Keep this one," Elliott said, putting his arm around her. "Let him be the Barefoot Bay Buck mascot. We can call him—"

"Stop." She cut him off with a harsh look and a sharp bark. "Don't do this anymore!"

"Do what?"

"Make me fantasize and imagine and dream and *want*. You're not real, Elliott A. Becker. You're not genuine. You're a fake. You're working me and toying with me and making me fall for you and then, wham, you'll be gone when the next investment or opportunity or lucky money-making scheme comes your way."

He still stared at her, a world of hurt in his eyes. "No, I won't, Frankie."

She turned away. "You will. Like everyone else, you'll…disappear." Like her parents. Like Nonno. Like any hope of having someone stay forever.

"Only if you want me to."

"I do!" she cried, hating the crack in her voice. "I want you to disappear. *Now*."

Without a word, he pushed up, the only sound the soft whimper of Isabella's relief and the rustle of hay under his feet. She didn't turn to watch him go, but listened to his footsteps through the shelter, the barks of her dogs, and goodbye nays from the girls.

She stayed very still, petting Isabella and the brand new babies, while the sound of his car engine started, then grew quiet as he left her.

Ozzie came prancing over, barking his displeasure.

"I know, Oz." She kept him away from the stall with one hand, but looked into his sad brown eyes. "I liked him, too." Too much.

Ozzie made a soft harrumph and flattened on the hay, every bit as broken and bereft as Frankie.

147

Chapter Twelve

Twenty-one.

There were now twenty-one little cotton balls lined up along Frankie's soap-making counter. Three weeks' worth of fragrant messages.

But nothing else.

Agnes and Lucretia flanked her, their pygmy bodies pressed up against Frankie's knees as she neatly sealed the last of the soap bars for the meeting with Jocelyn that would start in less than an hour. Behind her, the doeling and buckling romped, still a little wobbly and high-pitched, alternating between crazy and exhausted every minute of the day.

She'd named the girl Daisy because of the flower-like white splotch on her forehead. And the buck? She hadn't named him yet. Still unsure if she could keep two of them here because of the complicated logistics of two bucks on the same little farm, she refused to let herself fall for him by giving him a name.

She just thought of him as Becker's boy, and that made her think of Becker, and that made her...not completely sad but damn close.

She picked up the cotton ball that had arrived today,

hand-delivered by special messenger, who brought one every day when Frankie finished the morning milking. Each one arrived in a plastic box with nothing but a tiny piece of paper bearing a few words.

So now she had twenty-one obscure, impossible messages from Elliott Becker. Was he trying to tell her something or just help her with the soap fragrances he knew she was creating for Casa Blanca?

Hard to say, but with every new arrival, her heart softened ever so slightly. She picked up the one that had arrived today and sniffed it.

The first few had come with names that recapped so much of their time together. The good parts, when they were falling hard and fast. *First Kiss. Intimate Moments. Moonlight Madness. Secret Whispers.*

The following week, his messages reflected the state of her heart with uncanny accuracy. *Tender Ache. Empty Arms. Lonely Days. Sleepless Nights.*

What was he trying to tell her with the complex fragrances and cryptic messages? Each one confused and intrigued and delighted her. No phone calls. No texts. No letters or flowers or emails or postcards.

Just glorious fragrances and mystifying messages.

And this week, the tone had changed again. Now, instead of angst, she got...*Sweet Anticipation. Hopeful Heart. Counting Hours.* And, then, today's, the most perplexing of them all.

Coming Home.

Home? Her heart raced, but she calmed herself with a slow, deep inhale of the sweetest fragrance he'd sent to date. A marvel of vanilla and oak blend, like nothing she'd ever made before.

Maybe he was sending messages, maybe he was

trying to help out, maybe he was the world's most creative groveler. She didn't care. The fragrances and names were a gift she gladly accepted. She'd re-created every one up until today's, producing a total of twenty new fragrances and beautifully packaged sets of soap she'd wrapped and ribboned and turned into a celebration of romance. Jocelyn would love these, use these, and sell these like crazy.

She took a sniff of Coming Home. She'd make that, but maybe save it for herself.

Putting the last of the baskets in the back of her truck, she absently ran a hand over Lucretia's soft neck, rewarded with a loopy goat smile.

"Wish me luck, girls."

Before she left she checked on Daisy and…that guy really needed a name. Black and shiny as his father, the little buck had a gleam in his eyes and a constant need for affection. She shouldn't get attached, but she reached down and gave him a hug anyway, his baby fur tickling her cheek.

"You know I'm going to end up calling you Becker and will regret it every time I have to say the name."

He whined noisily and stomped his tiny hooves in response. A chorus of goats guided her to the pen gate, but before she left, Frankie stood and looked at her little homestead. Her home. It was, now. And it was time to build La Dolce Vita. The resort would help get people over here, and she'd already talked to the gardener and head chef about using her goat's milk and selling that, too. First step, today's sale. Then tonight, she'd be…

Coming Home.

Alone.

She climbed in the truck and drove to Casa Blanca,

150

trying to focus her thoughts on the meeting ahead with Jocelyn, a woman she'd grown to like and trust in the past few weeks. Jocelyn had confided that her father was very sick, with advancing Alzheimer's, and her dream was for him to live long enough to see her baby. She'd also shared the story of how she'd forgiven her father for the sins of his past, making Frankie think long and hard about letting go of the misplaced anger she harbored against her parents.

They'd only been trying to do the right thing for her. She had to stop blaming them and their careers for dying and remember that they loved her fully and wholly.

The parking lot of the resort was packed, but that wasn't so much of a surprise. Business in the restaurant, Junonia, was booming, and this late in the day, the promise of a gorgeous sunset brought people all the way from the mainland for cocktails and beach walks. Still, she'd never seen it quite this packed. She had no choice but to use the valet service, otherwise she would have had to cart all those baskets across the lot.

"Here for the event, ma'am?" the valet asked as he opened her door.

"I'm meeting with Jocelyn Palmer, the manager of Eucalyptus."

"No problem, we'll park it for you."

"I need to get those baskets out of the back."

He helped her take them into the lobby, which was even more crowded than the parking lot, with dozens milling about, sipping champagne, and waiters carrying trays of more flutes and food.

"Is there a wedding today?" she asked the valet.

"No, a press conference. ESPN is here!" His eyes bugged with excitement. "There's some big baseball thing. You should see who's here, too. Couple of Yankees, people from the MLB, and…" He leaned closer and looked side to side before lowering his voice. "Nathaniel Ivory is here."

"Oh." She had to get out of here before she saw Becker. Still holding one of the baskets with two hands, she shouldered through the crowd to the double doors of the spa, struggling to figure out a way to get the door and not put down the basket.

Suddenly, someone came up behind her and grabbed the oversized brass handle for her.

The tightening in her chest squeezed until it crushed her heart as she stared at the hand in front of her. Long, strong, tanned, masculine, and far too familiar. A hand she'd held. A hand that had touched her. A hand that—

"Let me help you."

She gathered her wits, took a breath, and looked up to meet the very ebony eyes that haunted her every night.

"You already have," she said, hoisting her basket a little higher, as if it could protect her from the impact of his size and proximity. "Thanks for the poetic and creative ideas."

"I have one more." His voice was low and intimate, and just a little too close for comfort.

"I got today's, thank you."

"One more creative idea. Would you like to hear about it?" Without waiting for her response, he took the basket she carried and opened the door for her, using his whole body to usher her in.

"I would not," she said crisply, walking to the wide receptionist desk. "Hi, I have an appointment with Jocelyn Palmer."

Elliott was right next to her in an instant. "She can't meet with you now. But I can."

The receptionist let out a soft laugh. "Is this the woman you've been asking about?" she asked him.

"This is the one. The one and only."

A totally unwanted and undeniable thrill danced through Frankie as she managed a smile. "But I have an appointment with Jocelyn."

He turned to the other woman and lifted his brows expectantly, giving her a moment to reply.

"Um, I'm afraid she's canceled that, Ms. Cardinale."

"What?"

"Her husband has asked her to be part of the announcement, and they're doing a walk-through meeting in the private dining room right now." She frowned at Elliott. "Aren't you supposed to be in there?"

"I have my own meeting." He put a possessive hand on Frankie's shoulder and gestured toward the hallway that led to the backrooms of the spa. "This way."

She refused to move. "I'm not..." She gave a pleading look to the receptionist. "Can I at least talk to Jocelyn?"

"I'll try and reach her."

"You do that," Elliott said. "We'll be in her office."

He pressed on her back, and Frankie let out a sigh, going toward the doorway she knew led to the spa manager's office.

"Why are you doing this?" she asked.

"I have to show you something." He opened Jocelyn's office door and guided her to the round table in the corner.

For a second, all she could do was stare at what was

on the table. It was like...nothing she'd ever seen. She stood there and drank in every precious detail of a three-dimensional model of...a goat farm? She fell into the closest chair, a fine chill exploding over her skin as she tried to process the absolute perfection of the work.

"It's part of today's announcement." He stood behind her and placed his hands on her shoulders.

Questions bubbled up, but before she could ask anything she had to just look at it. Someone brilliant had designed this, someone who'd managed to climb into her imagination—and Nonno's—and create something that was as beautiful as it was functional.

"It's a 3-D scale model, but—"

She held her hand up to silence him, not wanting any more information while she absorbed what was in front of her. Acres of land, with a two-story. stone farmhouse that looked like it had been plucked from the hills of Tuscany perched in one corner, looking out over the expanse of a complex that included a large round pen, a bright red shelter and workhouse, and a precious little storefront surrounded by wooden benches and shade trees. A closed-off petting area filled one side and behind it, a series of larger pens, with a hand-painted sign above them that read: *The Official Mascots of the Barefoot Bay Bucks!*

"That's what we're calling the team," he said, adding some pressure to her shoulders as if he could underscore the importance of that. "So we'd love to expand the whole stadium complex to include this visitors' attraction, which we think the families and kids will love."

"It's..." She reached out and touched the gentle curve of a window dormer on the house, something so precious and inviting, it twisted her heart. "Dreamy." In fact, it was right out of one of her dreams.

"Do you like it?"

She looked up, over her shoulder. "I assume that's a rhetorical question."

He laughed, coming down next to her, taking one knee so they were face-to-face. "You and your ten-dollar words, Francesca. Is this what you want to do with your land? Did I understand what you told me?"

She searched his face, only slightly more appealing to her eyes than the work of art next to her. "Is this supposed to go on my land?"

"That's up to you. This is an optional piece of a master plan that's being announced in"—he glanced at his watch—"fifteen minutes. We can leave this out and build everything to the west of your property, with absolutely no infringement on your land at all. Or..." He took her hands, and only then did she realize she was shaking. All over. "This can be part of the plan."

"Whose plan?"

"Our plan, Frankie." He lifted her hand and pressed her knuckles to his lips, closing his eyes like a wave of relief and joy rocked him. "God, I missed you."

She tried to swallow, but a lump the size of, well, a baseball, filled her throat.

"Frankie, I don't know any way..." He opened his eyes, which were as shockingly damp as hers felt. "I don't know how to tell you in any other way how sorry I am that I hurt you and how much I want"—he inhaled a steadying breath—"a chance to be with you. A chance to hold you and make promises to you and to be completely real with you."

She'd dreamed of this moment, hadn't she? In fact, it was very possible she was dreaming right now.

Just like with Nonno.

Ignoring the quivering of her hand, she lifted her fingers to his face and grazed the rough shadow of whiskers and the smooth curve of his full lower lip. "You seem pretty real," she whispered.

Under her fingertips, he smiled. "I am. And so's this idea. Real and right and..." He blinked and glanced toward the model. "It feels like home."

Her heart slipped around and fell to her stomach. "My home."

"Our—"

She pressed on his lips to stop him. "Don't."

"Why not?"

"Because it will hurt too much when it's over."

"It doesn't have to be over, ever."

"Stop," she pleaded. "You're so good with words, with saying exactly the right thing, with...pretend."

"Said the woman who pretended to be dirt-poor."

"I did not," she shot back. "I'm just me. You never asked for a bank statement, so I never told you. You know how I feel about money. It's the source of all my pain."

He leaned closer, his expression warm and sincere. "Then let me be the source of all your pleasure. And contentment. And whatever else you want in the world, Francesca. Please."

She managed a slow but shaky breath. "What are you asking from me? Permission to use my land?"

"We want you to be a partner in the project. And you'll be in charge of..." He reached under the board that held the model and pulled out a miniature banner that he stabbed into the soft, fake grass. "La Dolce Vita."

The Sweet Life. And wouldn't it be? Couldn't it be? With—"Did you say a partner?"

"I sure did."

She swallowed, her mouth surprisingly dry. "A business partner?"

He took her face in his hands and held her head perfectly still so she couldn't look anywhere but right into his eyes. "A life partner."

The door pushed open, and they both backed away to see Jocelyn, who was equally surprised to find her office full—with a man on one knee. "Oh...oh, did I...Frankie! Did you see what's going on in the lobby?"

Frankie stood, vaguely aware she still held Elliott's hand as he came up with her. "The press conference?"

"Your soaps! Someone opened the baskets you brought and thought they were party favors, and they've been passed around to everyone, and people are asking for more."

"Well, I guess that's—"

"Good marketing," Elliott supplied. "Sorry we stole your office, Joss."

"Not a problem, but your team is looking for you, Elliott. They're ready to start the announcement."

He turned to Frankie, anticipation brightening his eyes. "Are you coming? We can easily bring this and add it to the plan." He lifted the corner of the model to show how light and portable it was.

She opened her mouth to answer, but nothing came out. Should she risk everything on him again? "I don't know," she said, her voice rough. "I need...time. To think."

He pulled her closer, putting a light kiss on her forehead. "The offer is real. Everything is."

With that, he left, nodding to Jocelyn on his way out.

"Please tell me I didn't just interrupt The Big Moment," she said with an awkward laugh when he was gone.

"No, *a* big moment, not *the*." She gave herself a little hug, smiling at the other woman. "I don't know what to do," she admitted, surprising herself with her honesty.

"You want advice from a pregnant woman who's watched her three best friends fall in love like dominoes and did the same thing right after she stepped foot on this island?"

"Really?"

"Kick off your shoes and—"

Frankie held up a hand. "Got it. But…" She turned to the model. "He's so big on grand gestures, I never know if he's real or not."

"Oh, he's real. My husband has been in on a lot of the planning sessions, and he's told me how Elliott's fought for this. The Barefoot Bay Bucks was his idea, and he's paid gazillions to buy land around and adjacent to yours so no one had to touch your farm. And he's masterminded this charity program where a portion of every game ticket sold is going to a foundation he's starting called No Kidding that gives goats to families in Third World countries to help feed them with goat's milk."

She just blinked at her. "I've created a monster. In a good way."

Jocelyn laughed. "He's the butt of their every joke, but he loves it because he loves…" She caught herself. "He's a good guy," she added softly.

"I'm scared." The admission came right from the heart and didn't even surprise her. She was scared. Scared to love and lose again. Scared to trust and believe and hope.

Jocelyn stepped forward with outstretched hands. "You wouldn't be human if you weren't a little afraid. You can't protect yourself from never getting hurt, Frankie. If you try to do that, you'll never live. You'll never know." She gave Frankie a light hug. "I'm going out to the pavilion to watch the show. Want to come?"

"I'll stay here, if you don't mind."

"Think about it," Jocelyn said as she left Frankie alone.

After a moment, Frankie sat down again and stared at the model. It was like he'd climbed into her imagination and her heart and made her dreams come true.

"All *our* dreams, *piccolina*."

She whipped around at the sound, but the room was empty. The door was closed. And she was alone. "Nonno?" A shudder passed through her, and then a complete and thorough sense of peace and comfort.

But there was nothing, no one, not even a flutter in the air. Only the fine line between her imagination and what was *real*.

And then she knew what she had to do.

Chapter Thirteen

Elliott stood to the far side of the makeshift platform stage, next to Zeke and their fourth partner, Garrett Flynn, the three of them content to stay out of the limelight. The media weren't here for anyone but Nate Ivory, who, despite his proclaimed distaste for the spotlight, looked damned at home with a ton of it pouring over him.

The patio of Junonia was full with media and VIP guests, but Elliott's gaze stayed locked on the doors leading into the spa, his every breath strained as he waited for Frankie. All he wanted was a chance to show her what he was made of, what he could be.

But she stayed conspicuously out of sight.

He turned back to the reason they were here, the news of the Barefoot Bay Bucks. In answer to a question about management, Nate explained that he'd be living in Barefoot Bay and supervising the building of the stadium complex and managing the day-to-day logistics of starting a new minor-league team.

"I'm planning to be here a lot, too," Zeke said under his breath. "You?"

Elliott slid him a glance. "Not sure yet."

Zeke tracked his gaze to the spa door. "Did you actually beg?"

"Like a pathetic dog."

"One knee?"

"Till I had carpet burn."

"I can't believe she didn't go for the goat-farm idea."

Elliott blew out a noisy breath. "I messed up so bad, Zeke."

"You never know."

But he knew. He'd taken his usual, easy, effortless shortcut to get what he wanted, and it had cost him everything. He wasn't quite sure when he'd become so certain that Frankie Cardinale was everything, but it didn't matter. She was, so now he had nothing.

Finally, the questions turned away from Nate and back to the Bucks, and the stadium complex, and that brought Will Palmer front and center. Thanks to him, they were well connected with the resort, including the talented architect who'd built the place, Clay Walker. Together with Clay, they answered questions about logistics and environmental concerns, and how to handle the increased traffic this would bring to the island.

All the while, Elliott watched that door, his heart sinking like the sun behind him, lower and lower as each minute ticked by.

"I have to talk to her," he murmured to Zeke.

"Now?"

"I have to." Before Zeke could stop him, he shot to the side of the patio deck, trying to stay inconspicuous as he hustled behind the crowd and jogged down the stairs. He pulled the door and swore softly to find it locked. Without giving it another thought, he set off to find another way back into the resort, determined and certain now. It took a full five minutes to work through the crowd, back into the lobby, and to the front entrance of the spa.

Without even glancing at the receptionist, he marched right into the management offices, yanked the door open, and…stared at nothing.

She was gone and so was the model of La Dolce Vita.

For a second, he couldn't breathe, his pulse slamming against his temples, a band of disappointment clamping his chest. Shaking his head, he stood in the doorway and let the power-punch of regret and disappointment pound him.

He didn't want to live without her, but she clearly felt differently. Taking one step inside, he fought a sting in his eyes and a lump in his throat.

Next time he'd be real. No matter how hard it was, he'd never fake his way through anything again. If nothing else, that's what a week on the goat farm had taught him.

Swallowing the pain and his pride, he turned and retraced his footsteps, all the way through the lobby, into the restaurant, and back to the deck where he heard…

A woman's voice through the microphone?

Stepping into the fading sunshine, he peered over the heads of the guests, to see Nate, Garrett, and Zeke on the stage alongside…Frankie?

"I'm thrilled to partner with the project," she said into the microphone, her voice clear and strong and like music to his ears. "My grandfather was a founding father of this island, and I know he'd be over the moon to see a team named after his beloved animals and this wonderful visitors' center…"

Elliott shouldered his way forward, reaching the front just as Frankie pointed to the table they'd set up with the three-dimensional stadium complex model, this time with the addition of La Dolce Vita.

She met his gaze, smiling through eyes as misty as his felt right then and reached her hand out. "We've been waiting for you."

He stepped forward, taking her hand and joining his partners. All of them.

Nate leaned up to the microphone. "And now for what you've all really been waiting for—the exhibition game! You know we have players from five different Major League teams and our own softball team for a game of sandlot." He pointed to the beach where a large area had been cleared for a makeshift ball game. "And I do mean sand."

A cheer went up, mostly from the other guys on the Niners who'd come down for the event, but Elliott barely heard. Instead, he gripped Frankie's hand.

"Partner?" he asked.

"Not only that," she said with a smile, lifting her hand to slide on a baseball cap with a stylized N. "I qualify to play on your team."

He reached to hug her, but Nate gave his shoulder a slam. "No kissing. We gotta win this game."

"He hates to lose," Elliott told her. "So we'll kiss later."

"Damn right we will, Becker."

"Frankie! You did it!" A beautiful young woman sidled up to Frankie, her arms outstretched. "I'm so happy for you!"

Frankie hugged her, laughing. "Thanks for breaking the rules, Liza." She turned to Elliott. "You remember Liza Lemanski, the great unraveler of red tape."

In a flash, Nate was next to him, his focus on the beautiful blue-eyed brunette. "I like a woman who can unravel."

Liza didn't giggle or flush or toss her hair like most women when Nate Ivory zeroed in on them. Instead, she pinned him with a dead-serious look. "Good," she said. "Because I've come to do a little unraveling."

Elliott looked skyward and finally got his arm around Frankie, pulling her into him and taking her down to the beach. "What changed your mind?" he whispered when they were finally alone on the sand.

"Nonno."

"You think he would have liked the idea?"

"I know he does." She smiled up at him. "He told me."

"He did?" Elliott raised his brows. "What else did he say?"

She turned, the sunset behind her a golden glow, her dark hair falling over one eye under the ball cap, her smile lit up from deep in her heart. "You're the real deal."

He let out a sigh and pulled her into his chest. "I been trying to tell you that."

"I had to figure it out for myself." She kissed him long and hard, and rested her head on his shoulder. "You really want to be a goatherd, Becker?"

"You really want to spend your life with a billionaire, Francesca?"

She smiled up at him. "Yeah. Come on, let's play."

Arm in arm, they walked together toward home base.

Next up for The Billionaires of Barefoot Bay:

Scandal on the Sand

One more negative headline will cost Nate Ivory everything, so he's made a vow to stay out of trouble, no matter how difficult that can be for "Naughty Nate." But Liza Lemanski has some news that's not only scandalous...it is about to rock his entire world. Here's a sneak peek at *Scandal on the Sand*, the third novella in the **Billionaires of Barefoot Bay** trilogy!

~ EXCERPT ~

I t was her eyes. As soon as Nate caught a glimpse of the arresting color, somehow both impossibly ocean blue and bottle green, he had to talk to the woman, listening carefully as she was introduced to one of his friends.

"You remember Liza Lemanski, the great unraveler of red tape."

He didn't waste a second moving closer, getting a whiff of a barely-there citrus scent. "I like a woman who can unravel," he said with a wink.

"Good." When she turned to him, her turquoise gaze held no hint of playfulness. "Because I've come to do a little unraveling."

His friend made some kind of parting jab, reminding Nate that he was up third in the exhibition softball game that was about to start, but Nate's attention was on the beauty in front of him. "So, who's getting unraveled, blue eyes?" he asked.

"You."

Nice. "And I like a woman who doesn't mess around."

"That's not what I hear." She still wasn't smiling, making him wonder if the comment was a flirt or not. "We need to talk, Mr. Ivory."

That would be...*not.* Did he know her and forget those gorgeous eyes? Anything was possible, of course. With him, everything was possible. Or used to be.

How long would his past mistakes haunt him? Was he about to get an earful of how he'd made promises he'd never kept or taken phone numbers he'd never used or...worse? It could always be worse. Instantly, he felt his protective privacy walls rise like titanium barriers as he automatically reached for the sunglasses in his pocket.

"Sure, sure, let's talk after the game." Slipping them on, he took all the humor out of his tone and a step in the other direction.

She came with him, shaking back some long dark hair to make sure he could see she meant business. "Let's talk now."

"It'll only be three innings and then we're having a cocktail party at sea. We can unravel anything you want." He lifted his hand in a halfhearted wave goodbye.

"I prefer *now*."

Damn. He glanced around the large beachfront deck where he had just finished the press conference announcing the plan to launch a minor-league baseball team in Barefoot Bay. But no one came to his rescue. His business partners were already headed toward the sand for the softball game they'd put together to cap off the media event.

"Sorry, I gotta run. I'm batting cleanup."

"Yes, you are. Right this minute. With me."

Pushy little thing, wasn't she? Protected by reflective lenses, he let his gaze drift over her, lingering on fine cheekbones and lush lips that hadn't yet given him a real smile. Farther down, things got even better, with generous cleavage peeking out of a V-neck T-shirt and a tiny waist and soft curves under her jeans. She couldn't be five-four and a hundred and ten soaking wet.

"What's this about?" he asked, getting a sense that it *wasn't* about seeing her soaking wet, either.

"I need your signature."

"Oh." Relief washed through him as he let out the breath he'd been holding since he heard the edge in her voice. "You want an autograph?"

"No, I want your *signature*."

He didn't like the sound of that. "Listen, sweetheart, I have to play a ball game. So, later's better." Later, he'd be surrounded by his rec softball team and some pro ballplayers, safe from any accusations, suggestions, or sob story she might fling at him.

"Over here." She gestured toward an empty table that the wait staff of the Casa Blanca Resort & Spa had already cleared. Everyone had disappeared to the beach to watch the game.

Which was where he suddenly wanted very much to be.

"Whatever it is, make it fast." He purposely took all tease from his tone. She was hot, no doubt about it, but for some reason he smelled big trouble in this little package.

She responded by scraping a chair over the wooden deck as she pulled it out...*for him*. He stayed where he was while she took the other chair and opened up a large handbag.

"Okay...Liza." He rolled the name on his tongue, taking time to appreciate the sassy and sexy sound of it and wishing she were a little more of both.

"I really think you're going to want to be sitting down for this," she said.

"What do you have?" Irritation prickled his spine at her icy tone. Irritation and worry. He'd sworn on his life that there wouldn't be any more scandals, no more headlines, no more sexts that made their way to Perez Hilton's blog. Oh, that had been a bad week. The Colonel had *not* been amused.

She snapped a large manila envelope on the table.

"Pictures?" he guessed with a mirthless snort. "How original." Every stinking blackmailing female in a nightclub had their secret cell phone shots. Which was why he'd sworn off the club scene along with the rest of his far-too-active social life.

When she didn't answer, he ventured closer. "Oh, don't tell me, TMZ has offered five figures." He could only imagine what she had. "Let me guess. You've got 'Naughty Nate' bare-ass naked in Vegas or Cabo. He's got a joint in one hand and a fifth of Tito's in the other. Some dot-com billionaire's wife is grabbing his johnson, and they're about to fall into a hot tub with four more blondes."

Sickening that he could describe that situation a little too clearly. Swallowing a wave of self-loathing, he watched her slide a packet of papers onto the table, along with a spiral notebook.

What the—

"Nate! You're on deck!"

He ignored the announcement, hollered from the sand, instead dropping into the chair next to her.

"So, how much?" he demanded, a sixth sense already telling him what was going down here. The question went against everything he'd been taught as a member of a family with the iconic—and ironic—last name of *Ivory*. A family that was anything but pure and had trained all members that the first check was just that...the *first*. A blackmailer never went away.

But he absolutely refused to get embroiled in one more public mess and, damn it, if he had to pay to get rid of her, he would. Whatever it took to prove that he was worthy of the family name and...the chance to see that dark disapproval erased from his grandfather's eyes.

"I don't want money," she finally said.

Then what? Access to the Hollywood studio his older brother ran? A meeting with his other brother, the senator? Maybe insider-trading information from his cousin on Wall Street?

"Everybody wants something, Liza," he said on a sigh. Especially from an Ivory.

For the first time, the closest thing to a sweet expression settled on her lovely features. Her lips finally relaxed into a hint of a smile. Dark brows unfurrowed, and a slight blush of pink deepened her creamy complexion.

"Yes, everybody does want something," she whispered. "And I want you to sign this document." She slid the paper toward him. "And then I will go away and you can play softball and drink in Cabo with other guys' wives and have cocktails *under* the sea, for all I care."

She flattened him with a dead-eyed look. "Sign, and I promise you will never see or hear from me again."

He had to slide off his shades to read the paper, blinking at the legalese, his name typed neatly in the blanks. And…*Dylan Cassidy, age four.*

"Who's Dylan?"

"Your son."

The words slammed like a power-punch to his temple, and for a second he actually saw stars. A *kid*? He'd been so careful. His whole freaking adult life, he'd been so damn careful about this. Very slowly, he lifted his gaze from the page to her face, digging like a dog in dirt for a shred of a recollection of this woman, a date, a night, an encounter, a damn quickie in the back room of a party.

Nothing.

"I don't even remember you," he said, the words sounding as jagged as they felt. How wasted had he been to forget this girl?

"Of course you don't remember me," she said. "I've never met you."

"But…this…" He tried to focus on the paper again, but a slow fire of horror sparked in his gut and rolled up to burn his chest as the words stopped dancing in front of his eyes. *Voluntary Termination of Parental Rights.* "This isn't a paternity suit?"

"No, this is my guarantee that I can live in complete peace without an ax hanging over my head."

What the hell? "I'm confused. Do you mind explaining what you are talking about?"

"I want you to sign this so that I don't wake up some morning and find out the Ivory family is out to take Dylan away from me."

"You said he...we..." He let out a puff of pure frustration. "I don't get this at all. If I'm signing away rights to your child, how can I have never met you?"

"I'm not his mother." She nudged the paper closer. "Not that you care about her or have bothered to check, but his mother is dead, and I'm his legal guardian. And all you need to do is sign right there, and I'll handle the rest of the red tape. As you heard, I'm good at that."

Dead? Was she saying this boy was an *orphan*? Another cascade of unfamiliar emotions squeezed some air out of his lungs, but he forced himself to breathe and get to the facts, starting with the obvious. "Who is his mother?"

Her expression was total surprise, followed by a resigned shrug. "I suppose more than one woman has told you she's pregnant in your lifetime. Her name was Carrie Cassidy."

Slowly, he shook his head to say he'd never heard that name in his life. "What happened to her?" Maybe that would jog his memory.

"She was in a car accident a year ago and died almost instantly." She held out a pen. "Please. Make it easy on all of us."

Easy? Nothing about this conversation was easy.

She leaned forward and speared him with her jewel-toned gaze. "She left enough details about how you dumped her, penniless and pregnant, to fill a whole issue of the *National Enquirer*. Imagine the headline: *Nathaniel Ivory, Deadbeat Baby Daddy*."

It didn't take much of an imagination to visualize how well that issue would sell.

She was right about one thing—signing would be easy. Two scratches of a pen and he could go play softball and drink scotch and live his life. No scandal, no problems, no...

No way.

"I'm not signing anything."

Close. She was so close that every cell in Liza's body was quivering, but somehow she managed to keep her cool. Finally facing Nathaniel Ivory, after eleven months of planning for this moment, she wasn't about to let him know that her insides were mush and her heart was exploding against her ribs and she could throw up from the nerves. She couldn't let him know how much this mattered or that she was totally bluffing about the *Enquirer* because...she wouldn't dream of dragging Dylan through mud like that.

She was doing this *for* Dylan, who was everything to her.

"What's in that notebook?" Nate asked, attempting to reach for it, but she snatched it away.

"No, you don't."

"I knew you were lying." He spat out the accusation with disgust.

"I'm not lying!" She clutched the book, holding it to her chest. "You could take this and run. I'm not letting you have it."

"Run? Run where? To the beach? Who *is* this dead woman and what fiction did she write in that book? What proof do you have? Have you ever heard of DNA testing? Do you really think I'm going to sign something without answers? You think I can't smell the stink of your scam from a mile away?" The questions came at her like bullets from an automatic rifle, each one lodging in her throat and chest and gut. "Forget the pretend mother and bogus baby, what is *your* deal, Liza Lemanski?"

Oh, she'd been so close. She saw the moment he'd wavered and nearly signed the document. Almost but not quite there…like everything in her life. And now he thought she was a con artist. Great.

"My deal is that you sign this paper." *Stay on point, Liza. Don't let him sway you.*

"Why now?" he asked. "Didn't you say she died a year ago? And this alleged son is four? What took so long to collect your cash, huh?"

"I'm not…" She shook her head. "You told her you wouldn't help her, and I didn't know you were the father until she died and left me as his guardian. I'm not scared of you or your family like she was." A white lie, but she had to appear strong. "I want a clean slate as I start the formal adoption process, so, please"—she tapped the paper—"let me have that and that will be the end of this."

"And you come up to me at the end of a press conference and throw this at me?"

"I read in the local paper that you'd be here this morning and I…" Called in sick, grabbed the papers she already had prepared—working in the County Clerk's office did have its advantages—and put her plan into action.

"Why not approach my lawyer? That's how things like this are done."

"I thought it would be—"

"Easier to extort money."

"I don't *want* money." She fisted her hand, punching the air. "And I know you don't want a child."

"How do you know anything about me?"

Holding the brightly colored spiral notebook, she picked at the half-peeled $3.99 Ross price tag on the back. "It's all in here, your name, your description, your words to her. But when you read all that, I have to be sure this book is protected. It's all I have to prove my case."

"Then maybe you don't have much of a case."

"Oh, I have a case. And I have a child who..." *Looks a hell of a lot like you.* "Who I want to keep, without living in fear that someone is going to try to claim him."

"So you've said." He inched forward. A lock of chestnut hair fell over his brow, close to the golden-brown eyes that looked so much like...like Dylan's. "What do you *really* want, honey, because I don't believe a word you're saying."

Tiny beads of perspiration stung at her neck and temples, her cool slipping with each second that she had to face him. "I want that child. I want him safe and protected with me."

Something flickered in his eyes, a flash that went by so fast she wasn't positive she'd seen it, but she knew she'd hit some kind of emotional hot button.

"And you don't," she added, because what if *that* was the hot button she'd hit? What if he wanted a child? "It says so right here." She tapped Carrie's journal, maybe a little harder than necessary. "It says a lot of things about you that I don't think you want out in public."

Hollow threat, of course, but still she threw that trump card down again, hoping it would work. Surely a

174

man with his lifestyle, money, and famously documented inability to commit didn't want a child he'd fathered almost five years ago.

Did he?

"Hey, Nate!"

Startled at the man's voice, Liza turned to see Zeke Nicholas, one of the other men who'd been involved in the announcement today, jogging across the patio deck, impatience darkening his expression. "You missed your at bat, man. Come on!"

Nate held up his hand and shook his head.

"'Scuse me," Zeke said to Liza as he reached the table. "But I have to steal this heartthrob for just a—"

"Shut it, Zeke!" Fury sparked in Nate's eyes, but he didn't take them off Liza, making her certain his anger was not directed at his friend.

Zeke froze midstep. "Everything okay here?"

"We're fine," Liza said, seizing the opportunity. "I'm getting Mr. Ivory's autograph." Not that she had any real hope left that he'd sign, but maybe with his friend here, he'd buckle. It was worth a shot. "Right here, sir. And then you'll make the second inning."

His nostrils flared as he took a slow breath and shook his head. "You have to play without me, Zeke." Suddenly, he stood, gathering up the papers and the envelope in one swooping motion. "Liza and I are going somewhere more private."

She didn't move but glanced at Zeke, who seemed as surprised as Liza was. "So we should meet you on board the yacht later, for cocktails?"

Nate shook his head. "Sorry, the party's canceled. Come on, Liza." He reached for her hand, and when she didn't take his, he closed his fingers over her wrist to gently pull her up. "I can't wait one more minute to get you alone."

Zeke looked skyward. "So much for 'the new Nate.'"

"Go play softball," he said through clenched teeth. "I've got something more important to deal with."

With a stiff nod, Zeke left, but Liza held her ground. "I'm not going anywhere with you."

"We're not talking about this here, out in the open with staff running around. Any one of them could be recording this conversation on a cell phone."

She glanced at the busboy who openly stared at Nate as he slowed purposely by their table. He was right, of course. Everyone was interested in his business.

"Look." He leaned closer, the low tenor of his voice practically vibrating the air between them. "I don't know you or this kid or this Carrie character from Adam. But if you think I'm putting my name on anything without details and dates, along with legal, scientific, and medical proof, you're out of your mind. Let's go."

She pressed the notebook to her heart, a flimsy four-dollar shield against his billion-dollar onslaught. "I have all that. And there's no doubt of paternity."

He tried to usher her away from the table. "Oh, there's plenty of doubt. I'm not stupid, and I don't make mistakes when I mess around with strangers."

"You're calling her a stranger? Your lover for almost two months until you found out she was pregnant and dumped her?"

His eyes widened, then he shook his head with a soft, sarcastic laugh. "I've heard some pretty creative scams, honey, really, I have. But I gotta hand it to you. This is good. Innovative, complex, and ballsy." He had the nerve to give her a salacious grin and openly check her out from head to toe, sending a completely unwanted awareness through her. "And all wrapped up in a hot little package with sex-kitten eyes and my kind of rack. It's good, kid. It's good."

Sex kitten? Kid? His kind of *rack*?

What had Carrie been thinking when she fell for this tool? "Nothing about this is innovative or ballsy and, honestly, the story isn't that complex. Let me spell it out for you."

"Not here."

"Right here, and right now."

Another waiter walked by, slowing his steps, and glancing in their direction.

"Okay, okay," she finally gave in, walking with him off the deck to the beach, to the opposite side of where the game was being played. When they were completely out of earshot of anyone else, she took a breath of salt-infused air, mustering up momentum for her power-plea. But her sandals sank into soft sand, giving him even more of a height advantage.

She refused to cower.

"Listen to me," she said. "You can deny this all you want or pretend you never heard of her or claim you're too smart to make a mistake. But the facts are simple: Carrie had your child after you made it perfectly clear you wanted no part of a baby, and she spent three years in fear that you'd find her and claim him. She lived with me since she arrived in Florida, pregnant and unemployed, and became my best friend. She was killed by a drunk driver on I-75 a year ago and left me guardianship of her child, whom I plan to legally adopt and raise. I can't do that until I know for sure and certain you will never try to take him away from me. What's *ballsy* about that?"

"Where does the money come in?" he asked with no hesitation.

"I don't *want* money," she repeated on an exasperated sigh. Was that so hard for him to understand? "I want freedom and peace of mind and my…this…Dylan." She swallowed as she said his name. "I want Dylan." Safe, close, happy. That's what she wanted. "Honestly, that's all I've ever wanted since the day a cop showed up at my door and told me Carrie was dead."

He had the decency to at least feign sympathy. "Sorry, but…" He reached for the notebook, tugging it from her fingers. "Let me see that. Let me—"

Something slipped out of the pages, fluttering to the sand. He stooped down and snagged it as she did the same, their heads tapping lightly. He got the picture before she did, but Liza had a second to see it was the photo of Dylan she'd slipped into the back of the journal.

She reached for it, instantly protective, even of his photo. "That's—"

"Me," he finished, staring at it, still crouched down.

"No, I took that…" Her voice faded as she realized what he was saying. "Yeah, he looks like you. So much for an innovative and complex scam for money, huh?"

Staring at the photo, he let his backside drop onto the sand to sit. "He's an Ivory," he whispered, awe and disbelief and recognition making his voice thick.

She plopped down next to him. "What do you think I've been trying to tell you?"

"That changes everything."

Her heart plummeted. "How?"

"I have to…" He struggled with the words, and her

brain raced to fill in the blank. Meet him? Take him? Claim him? What did he have to do now that he didn't want to do years ago when Carrie told him she was pregnant?

He exhaled. "I have to see that journal. Somewhere completely private."

"We can walk on the beach."

He shook his head and pointed his thumb at the baseball game behind him. "They'll come after me. Where do you live?"

"Too far and…" She didn't want him there. "No, let's go inside and sit at a table or in the lobby."

He gave her a funny look, slowly shaking his head as he stood, still looking at the picture. "You don't understand. I can't do that. People know me. They take pictures. They approach me. Let's just…" He gestured for her to follow him. "I have an idea."

But she didn't move, looking up at him, feeling so small and helpless and frustrated and scared. "Are you going to take him from me?" she managed to ask.

He reached down and took her hand, his silence almost worse than if he'd said yes.

Enjoy a sneak peek at
Barefoot in White,
the first book in **The Barefoot Bay Brides** trilogy.

"This one…" Willow sniffed her phone. "Yep, this one smells…" She sucked in a breath so deep it quivered her nostrils. "…like a whole bunch of trouble."

"Her texts stink?" Gussie looked up from her place on the floor, where she sat surrounded by about a hundred different swatches of fabric.

"Like Limburger in the sun." Willow exhaled and scrolled through the last five messages from the high-maintenance bride-to-be, clearing her throat to imitate this ass-pain of a bride. "My MOH and I will arrive at Casa Blanca on the fourth to do a full resort inspection and interview the wedding planning team, please include all amenities, especially all spa treatments."

"So, no groom?" Gussie asked with a derisive snort. "Just the bride and maid of honor to do a resort review and planning session? Sounds like an excuse for a girls' weekend of pampering and freebies, then they'll probably end up holding the wedding at a different resort."

"I doubt she'll find a place that fast." Willow kept reading. "Oh, this is my personal favorite. 'Our villa must have two bedrooms and baths with direct ocean view.'" She rolled her eyes. "Can she not read a map of Florida to see that Barefoot Bay is on the Gulf of Mexico, not the Atlantic Ocean?"

"I don't know if she can read a map, but I can tell you from the swatches she sent, she's color-blind." She waved some flesh-toned material.

"Oh, yeah. How are you doing with her 'all tones of sand' color palette selections?"

Gussie lifted a section of pale lace, the material barely covering the purple bangs of today's colorful wig. "You call this a palette? I call it beige, a dull and dangerous state of mind."

"Told you. This…" She squinted at the bride's name again. "Misty Trew is trouble." Willow locked the screen and set the phone on her desk. "Not only does she come with no referral, but who chooses a destination resort a month before the wedding?"

"Someone pregnant," Gussie suggested.

"Or someone the last bridal consultant dropped."

"Or someone"—the third member of the Barefoot Brides wedding planning team popped into the office doorway, her whole face covered by a giant gift basket—"with a mongo budget who can get what they want." Ari inched the basket to the side, her midnight eyes and jet-black hair contrasting the cream-colored bow around the cellophane wrapping. "Which is why I made this over-the-top welcome basket. Any volunteers to take it over to their villa? Bride and maid arrive in a few hours."

Willow pushed back and stood. "I'll go. I need the exercise."

Ari choked softly. "Says the woman who ran two miles this morning."

"Should have done four," Willow said as she took the basket, eyeing the mouthwatering contents. "Especially if I knew I'd be left alone with this box of truffles." She caressed the cellophane, giving a playful gasp when her fingers found an open seam. "Ooh, easy access, too."

"As if you'd touch a truffle," Ari teased.

"I have my moments. And our bride-to-be has a long list of demands, er, requests she sent, so I better make sure Artemisia is fully stocked right down to the Rosa Regale champagne that is, and I quote, '*The only thing I can possibly drink.*'"

"Spike it with Prozac while you're over there," Gussie suggested.

Laughing, Willow gathered the basket to her chest and headed out of the Casa Blanca Resort & Spa administration area where Barefoot Brides had its one-office headquarters. The upscale resort hummed with the activity of a typical Friday morning, gearing up for a busy weekend in Barefoot Bay.

Outside, the sun was high enough to make the gulf— *not the ocean*—sparkle turquoise, the water laced with white froth on a picture-perfect late-April morning. Bright yellow umbrellas spilled over the sand like lemon drops in the sunshine.

Willow chose the shady red-brick path that cut through the resort and led to each of the private villas, all named for different North African flowers in keeping with the Moroccan-inspired architecture. With each tap of her feet on the walkway, she let herself slip deeper in love with this piece of paradise.

They had to make this work, no matter how many high-maintenance brides put them through the wringer. Pooling their individual wedding consultant businesses to form Barefoot Brides had been her idea. The three of them moving here to run destination weddings at Casa Blanca was not only a unique selling point for clients...it was the key to Willow's personal happiness.

And she was happy, she reminded herself, humming a little, as though that soundtrack would prove the very thought to be true. So very happy and healthy and three thousand miles from California. New woman, new life, new everything.

Happy, happy, happy. The humming might be a little over-the-top, though.

Instead, she inhaled the briny bay air, stopping at the wrought iron gate that opened to Artemisia. Positioned on a rise, and angled so that the patio and pool faced the Gulf of Mexico, this butter-yellow villa was one of Willow's favorites on the property. Setting the basket on the terra cotta steps that led up to the front door, she pulled her resort ID that doubled as a master key out of her pocket, unlocked the door, and scooped up the goodies to go inside.

The living area was darkened from sunshades on the windows, cool and quiet, with the welcoming aroma of sweet gardenias left by the Casa Blanca cleaning staff. Heading to the kitchen, Willow froze mid-step at the sound of...was that running water? No. A footstep? She listened for a minute, heard nothing, then—

"Will ya...will ya...be my girl?"

Singing. Someone was singing. Well, more like howling. Woefully off-key.

"Gotta know if it's real, gotta know it's forevah!"

Willow's heart dropped so hard and fast the basket almost went with it. Was this some kind of joke? *That song*? That crappy, tacky, mess of metal that...that *pretended* to be a love song and paid for college and cars and everything else she'd had?

No one at this whole resort, on this island, or, hell, in the whole state of Florida, except for Ari and Gussie, could possibly know—

"No foolin' around, for worse or for bettah!"

Son of a bitch, who'd found her out? Did Ari or Gussie tell someone that Willow's father was a rock 'n' roll household name? They'd *promised* not to.

Gripping the basket so tight she could crack the wicker, she marched into the hallway that separated the two bedrooms, calling out, "Excuse me!"

"Will ya...will ya...be my..."

"Hey!" She lowered the basket to peer over the top and...oh. *Oh.*

Back.

Ass.

Muscles.

Ink.

Ass again. It deserved a second look.

"*Girrrrl!*" Tanned, muscular arms whacked the air, and a dark head of wet hair shook, sending droplets all the way down to...oh, really, that rear end was the most beautiful thing she'd ever seen.

"Come and take it, don't ya fake it, we can make—"

She opened her mouth, but nothing came out. The words caught in her throat, lost as her gaze locked on the bare-naked man air-drumming like a raving lunatic in the middle of the bedroom, totally unaware she stood behind him.

"Luh-uuuuve..." He destroyed the note, and not in the good way her father intended when he wrote the song. No, Donny Zatarain would probably weep if he heard his signature rock anthem being butchered by this idiot wearing nothing but noise-canceling headphones.

"Excuse me!"

His arms never missed a beat of the drum solo she had memorized before she was five years old, each stroke tensing and bulging muscles she hadn't even known existed. She opened her mouth to call out again, but that was a waste of time. Anyway, this particular feast for the eyes was way too good to pass up.

"Will ya, will ya be my *girrrrrl*?"

But that song *had* to stop. She reached into the basket and grabbed the first thing her fingers touched: a nice ripe Florida orange. Yanking it out, she lobbed it as he hit the high C on "girl," except he didn't come anywhere near C, and the orange didn't go anywhere near him.

Still, he spun around, jumping into a wide, threatening stance, both arms out like a warrior ready to attack. She blocked her face with the basket, peeking through the top spray of cellophane, silently thanking Ari for choosing clear.

Whoa, that was a big…man.

"What the…" he muttered after a second, whipping off the headset. "I didn't hear you come in. You can put that down out there. Thanks."

She didn't move. Not even her eyes, which were riveted to…his…his…him.

"Thanks," he repeated, the word tinged with impatience. "You can leave now."

What if her client had come face-to-face with this? With that exposed…giant…breathtaking… She'd think this took "welcome package" to a whole new level.

"No, *you* can leave, because you are not in the right villa," she said.

He scowled. Well, she assumed he scowled. It was difficult to see his face because she couldn't stop looking at the rest of him.

"I'm in the right villa. Isn't this Art..Arte...some flower that starts with an A?"

Was she in the wrong place? No, of course not.

Get a grip, Willow. He was just a naked man—okay, an exceptionally stunning naked man—and she had a job to do here. Which was to get him out of the villa.

"Artemisia," she supplied, her arms starting to burn from holding the basket high enough to cover her face but still see. "And, yes, you *are* in the wrong villa, because we have guests booked to arrive soon, and you're not one of them."

He turned his hands skyward in a less threatening gesture, not that his hotter-than-a-thousand-suns body wasn't threatening enough. "Yes, I am," he said. "And if you will please turn around, miss, and leave that in the living room, we're cool."

"No, we are not cool." There was an understatement. "Because I'm pretty sure you have more, um, body hair than the bride or maid of honor we're expecting."

He took a step closer, and she hoisted the basket high enough to completely cover her face.

"Man," he said

"Excuse me?"

"I'm a man." With two hands, he lowered the basket. "As you've obviously noticed. *Man* of honor. Not *maid*."

The words registered, but not the meaning, because she was face-to-face with his broad chest and wide shoulders and a deep-purple tattoo of…oh, really? Was this God's idea of a joke? That was the earth and star on the cover of *Zenith*, the number-one best-selling Z-Train record of all time. "Really?"

"Really. I'm the man of honor in Misty Trew's wedding." His tone was a mix of waning tolerance and growing amusement.

She finally lifted her eyes, finally coherent enough to process what he'd said, and realize the mistake was hers. "I get it," she whispered, meeting cocoa-colored eyes as rich and inviting as the truffles in her arms, and a mouth that could be forgiven for whatever sour notes he'd hit with it, and…

Once more, the world slipped out from under her, this time because recognition nearly buckled her knees. "You're…" Her throat closed.

"The man of honor."

"No, you're…" The one who…the boy who…no, now the man who…crushed her spirit.

"A male version of the maid."

"You're…" Nick Hershey.

"Naked," he supplied, adding a slow, sexy, sinful smile. "But you're not."

She clung to the basket as if it were the last logical thing on earth because right now, it was. "I'm not…" How long had it been? Ten or eleven years since she'd lived in a dorm at UCLA? And he'd been right down the hall. "Thinking straight."

"Clearly." He laughed and reached for the basket. "Here, let me take your junk so you can stop staring at mine." Placing the basket on the dresser, he held up a hand. "Just a sec. I'll get your tip."

"No tip, I'm not with the resort." The rote answer fell

out of her mouth as he took a few steps, forcing Willow to stare some more at that round, hard handful of Nick Hershey's world-class ass before he disappeared into the en suite. "That ought to be illegal," she murmured on a sigh.

"So should breaking into a hotel room," he replied.

"I wasn't expecting...anyone. Or at least, not a man." Buck-naked. And she sure as hell hadn't been expecting the guy she'd tried to give her virginity to one slightly tipsy night after finals. *Tried* being the operative word, because he...

A dose of shame and a splash of self-pity mixed into a cocktail of humiliation, rising up to choke her. He'd turned her down cold and flat.

Willow rooted for a coherent thought, trying to center on the present. The bride was from New York. Nick was from California. How was it even possible that he was standing here in Mimosa Key, Florida?

It didn't matter. He was here, and a key member of the wedding party she was coordinating, so Willow would have to maintain professionalism and get control. She closed her eyes, willing her body and brain to get in line, the way she always did when she wanted to be stronger than whatever temptation or distraction threatened her well-honed control.

"So, you're a friend of Misty's?" she asked.

"Not exactly. Her brother is supposed to be here, but he's still deployed." He stepped back into the room, a towel wrapped around his hips, tied low, exposing a trail of dark hair that ran from his belly button down to his...no, no one could ever call what she'd just seen *junk*. "I'm doing him a favor and acting as Misty's second-in-command."

"She doesn't have a girlfriend to be the maid of honor?"

His brow quirked. "Have you met Misty?" he asked.

"No, not yet."

"Well, you'll understand when you see her. She's a model," he said, like that explained it. And, having been raised by one, it kind of did. "She's not exactly swimming in female companionship."

He crossed his arms and took another long, slow look at her, his gaze leaving a trail of heat, followed by goosebumps, and more heat. Still not even the slightest shadow of recognition. No surprise there.

Very few—actually none—of the people who knew her in college would recognize Willow Ambrose as Willie Zatarain. Not even someone who'd always said hello and made a point of being kind to her…but not *that* kind. Not kind or even drunk enough to sleep with a woman who outweighed him by more than a hundred pounds.

That was then, and this was…getting awkward.

"You know," he said, as if suddenly aware of how much time had passed while they looked at each other. "In the military, there's a rule that once you've seen someone naked, they get to see you naked."

Suddenly, a flash came back to her. Nick, friendly and even flirtatious when they were in college. His voice—at least when he wasn't singing—still had that smooth, silky quality that poured over her like hot fudge on cold ice cream. And like sundaes, he'd always been a temptation.

But Willow had long ago learned how to conquer temptations, hadn't she? "Good thing I'm not in the military, then. I get a pass."

The vaguest hint of disappointment darkened his eyes, giving her a surprising jolt of satisfaction. "Hey, can't blame a guy for trying. Lieutenant Nick Hershey." He extended his hand for a shake. "You don't work for the hotel, so are you one of the planner girls?"

"The planner girls?" She coughed a soft laugh, mostly to cover the certainty that he didn't remember her. The question was, should she refresh his memory? See the look of utter and abject shock on his face? Endure the questions, the litany of congratulations, and the embarrassment for both of them?

"Sorry, that sounded demeaning as shit, didn't it? I meant are you working for Misty as her wedding consultant?"

"Yes." She finally lifted her hand to slide into his, fighting a shudder when his warm, large fingers closed over hers.

"And you're…" he prompted.

"I'm…" *A girl you knew a long time ago.* Not that she could blame him. Most days, she didn't recognize herself. "Willow Ambrose."

"Willow." He let the word roll around on his lips, tasting it, nodding as if he liked it a lot, smiling as though meeting her for the first time. Well, wasn't that why she'd ditched the shortened nickname and lopped off her world-famous last name?

"The pleasure is…well, I guess the initial pleasure was yours." He winked, and it hit her heart like a red-hot spark.

"Not the singing part," she teased.

He laughed, a low rumble in his chest that she *knew* could curl toes, melt hearts, and vacuum up phone numbers. "I suck, I know. But that's how I relax.

190

Does your job mean I'll be seeing a lot of you this weekend?" The little bit of hope in his voice tweaked her heart, still not grasping the fact that *he* was flirting with *her*.

"Depends on how much wedding planning you and the BTB are going to do."

"BTB? Wait, don't tell me. Bride That Bitches?"

It was her turn to laugh. "Bride To Be, but your version is often dead-on, too. I thought you and Misty weren't going to be here for a few hours."

"We came from different places, and I got bumped to an earlier flight, and she's...somewhere." He put his hands on his narrow hips, the move accentuating his chest and pecs and stunningly cut abs. "Want to show me around until she gets here?"

Could she...not tell him? The thought landed in her head with a thud. It would be dishonest not to tell him they'd known each other a dozen years...and a hundred and twenty pounds ago.

Except, he'd known Willie Zatarain, the fat girl in Sproul Hall who had few friends and famous parents. He didn't know Willow Ambrose. And by the way he was looking at her, he wanted to.

The powerful, dizzying, irresistible pull of temptation tugged at her insides. This time, just this one time, temptation kicked her ass.

"Yes," she said softly. "I'll show you around."

The Complete Barefoot Bay Series
by Roxanne St. Claire

All of the stories in this contemporary romance series take place in and around the fictional setting of Barefoot Bay, Florida. Each story stands alone but characters will reappear to surprise and delight readers! All books are available in print and digital versions. For links, exerpts, and character profiles, visit www.roxannestclaire.com.

The Barefoot Bay Quartet – full length novels
Barefoot in the Sand (Lacey and Clay)
Barefoot in the Rain (Jocelyn and Will)
Barefoot in the Sun (Zoe and Oliver)
Barefoot by the Sea (Tessa and Ian)

The Barefoot Bay Billionaires Trilogy – novellas
Secrets on the Sand (Mandy and Zeke)
Seduction on the Sand (Frankie and Elliott)
Scandal on the Sand (Liza and Nate)
The Barefoot Billionaires (an anthology that contains
all three novellas in one boxed set in print and digital)

The Barefoot Brides Trilogy – full length novels
Barefoot in White (Willow and Nick)
Barefoot in Lace (Gussie and TJ)
Barefoot in Pearls (Ari and Jason)

Prior to writing the Barefoot Bay series, Roxanne wrote romantic suspense in two popular series, and several stand alones. All titles are still available in digital versions and many are available in print.

The Guardian Angelinos (Romantic Suspense)
Edge of Sight
Shiver of Fear
Face of Danger

The Bullet Catchers (Romantic Suspense)
Kill Me Twice
Thrill Me to Death
Take Me Tonight
First You Run
Then You Hide
Now You Die
Hunt Her Down
Make Her Pay
Pick Your Poison (a novella)

Stand-alone Novels (Romance and Suspense)
Space in His Heart
Hit Reply
Tropical Getaway
French Twist
Killer Curves
Don't You Wish (Young Adult)

About The Author

Roxanne St. Claire is a *New York Times* and *USA Today* bestselling author of more than thirty novels of suspense and romance, including three popular series (*The Bullet Catchers*, *The Guardian Angelinos*, and *Barefoot Bay*) and multiple stand-alone books. Her entire backlist, including excerpts and buy links, can be found at www.roxannestclaire.com.

In addition to being a six-time nominee and one-time winner of the prestigious Romance Writers of America RITA Award, Roxanne's novels have won the National Reader's Choice Award for best romantic suspense three times, and the Borders Top Pick in Romance, as well as the Daphne du Maurier Award, the HOLT Medallion, the Maggie, Booksellers Best, Book Buyers Best, the Award of Excellence, and many others. Her books have been translated into dozens of languages and are routinely included as a Doubleday/Rhapsody Book Club Selection of the Month.

Roxanne lives in Florida with her husband and two teens, and can be reached via her website, www.roxannestclaire.com or on her Facebook Reader page, www.facebook.com/roxannestclaire and on Twitter at www.twitter.com/roxannestclaire.

Made in the USA
Charleston, SC
30 October 2014